YER BLUES

D1823995

YER BLUES

Othniel Smith

DEDICATED TO:

RAYMOND SMITH
(1970-1997)

JOHN PEEL
(1939-2004)

CHAPTER ONE

Perhaps a good place to begin is with Jase and Dai, sitting on their favourite bench, up on the hill, Jase facing the greyness of the town, and Dai gazing blankly at the luxuriant expanse of rolling green valley. It's six-thirty on a misty morning, the day after the news has broken that John Peel has died, and the boys, not for the first time, are sharing a sorry-looking spliff.

Another suitable starting-point might occur two and a half hours previously, in the midst of one of their infamous jam-sessions, with Dai crashing about on his drum-kit, and Jase alternately finessing and flailing at his cherished olive-green Fender Telecaster copy, in Dai's mother's suitably soundproofed garage, old mattresses not being hard to come by in these here parts.

When they started, years before, Dai and Jase used to tape them, listening afterwards, and suggesting, all giggly through the smoke, that they ought to send them to John Peel. Except that they knew that he'd have realised that they were just messing about, and that there was no integrity in them.

"He does play stuff where people are just pissing around, like, I've heard him."

"Sure. And he plays stuff where people have sent it in 'just to see if John Peel will play it on the radio'. But he always knows. And if he likes it, he'll play it, and if he doesn't he won't. Simple as." Jase is the sensible one.

"Yeah, but… National Radio One, like. The BBC!"

In between then and now, though, Dai has been on national radio, and found it not to be a very big deal, perhaps because, at the time, he was preoccupied. The band was a local one with a record deal, a reputation for living the rock'n'roll lifestyle, and a high turnover of drummers. Dai had not only played with the Independent Youth Jazz Ensemble of Wales between the ages of 14 and 17, but he was also a trained motor mechanic, which enhanced his usefulness on the road. His four-month stint took in the band's third single, and the summer festival season.

"The trouble with the rock'n'roll lifestyle is that these days, everybody's doing it. Especially round here. Getting ridiculously off your face on a regular basis, beating up your mates, not getting anything done – the Welsh invented the rock'n'roll lifestyle!" This is Jase, attempting, unsuccessfully, to comfort Dai after he had been kicked out of the band, just as they were about to board a 'plane for America, due to the heroin inexpertly concealed in his toilet bag.

Jase had emerged from his own drugs hell a year or so earlier. The curse struck around about the time he should have been going to university, thus leaving him without a future. Nowadays, he delivers curries for Mr and Mrs Khan, which doesn't pay much above the minimum wage, but at least he doesn't have to check in till 5.30 in the evening. Plenty of time to sleep, and practise his guitar. Not much time to brood over his non-existent social life.

Suggestion for another starting-point:- Dai sticking the blunt end of an HB pencil in his ear, just to see how far it will go. This is a little over seventeen years ago, on their first day in Miss Gwilym's class at primary school, with Jase and Dai placed together right at the back, since they were both late; Jase because his mother had got the days confused, and Dai because he'd had a puff on one his dad's cigarettes in the middle of a sleepless night, and had vomited all over his breakfast. Dai does the thing with the pencil to get Jase's attention, because Jase's mother has told him not to mix with bad company, and Dai looks like bad company. It is left to Jase to raise his hand, and get permission to accompany the confused-looking Dai on the first of many, many visits to the school nurse. They have been best friends ever since.

"We've got to do it, Dai, man. We've got to finally do it."

Dai chuckles to himself. "Sorry, Jase, I... I love you and everything, but... not in that way."

This is them, back on the bench, ears still ringing from their Peel Memorial Thrash-athon.

"We've got to take this music thing seriously. I mean... it's all I've got."

"Been there. Done that." Dai is still smarting from his brush with the biz, even though he is agonisingly aware that he is solely to blame for his fall. "Not all it's cracked up to be."

"Yeah, but you were a paid employee, Dai. You weren't doing your own thing, with your real mates. I mean... what do you want to do with your life, Dai?"

Dai doesn't reply. He knows that Jase knows that he doesn't really look very far beyond his next fix.

"Well I know what I want. I want to be a pro."

"With a face like that?"

Jase winces, slightly. He is sensitive about his appearance. He is tall, skinny, and awkward, and his year and a half of heavy drug abuse did little for his complexion. More than one person has remarked that he'd be better suited to the delivery of pizzas than vindaloos, since, on a bad day, his face could pass for a pepperoni special with extra cheese. He'd only ever got any action, during his teenage years, by hanging out with the more conventionally handsome (in a bright-eyed Valleys wide-boy kind of way) Dai, and copping off with Dai's temporary girlfriends' hangers-on, occasionally impressing them by being able to compare them with women from old films:- "You look a bit like that Gloria Grahame in 'It's a Wonderful Life' - if you lost a few pounds, like."

"I want to be a professional musician." Dai will not be swayed from his path. "I know I'm good enough."

"Being good enough isn't good enough, Jase. Any monkey can learn to play an instrument. Look at me." Dai sighs, self-dramatising.

"Yeah, I know. It's about creating your own material. And I'm crap at writing songs."

"I don't know. I quite like your Radiohead one. And your Nirvana one. Ooh – and your R.E.M. one's even better than the original, in my book."

Jase cannot help but give way to a pained smile. "You would appear, David, to have pinpointed the flaw in my cunning plan."

But Dai is no longer listening. In the middle distance, he has spotted two figures clad in fluorescent pastels. Unlike most habitual track-suit wearers in the vicinity, they are indulging in strenuous exercise. As they spot Jase and Dai, the shorter one slaps his compatriot on the arm, and they change direction, sprinting towards the bench.

"Shit." Teg and Bumpy are not Jase's favourite people. And since he forsook the hard drugs, he has fallen out of favour with them, as well.

"Alright boys?" Teg is barely out of breath, unlike his bear-shaped bodyguard-cum-bedmate.

"Teg. Bumpy."

"Lovely morning. That rolling mist. Fucking poetry, it is." Teg sees himself as something of an aesthete, on account of his fondness for BBC costume dramas. "Almost makes you believe in God."

"Not a card-carrying Jesus-freak, then, Teg?" Jase refuses to look the older man in the eye. "You do surprise me."

"Don't get me wrong – I respect the idea of faith. It's just that there's so many people what use it as an excuse to act like arseholes, know what I mean?"

"And you prefer to cut out the middle man, eh?"

Bumpy makes a move of the kind which seems destined to result in the bulk of Jase's head being torn from parent body, but Teg raises an arm to restrain him. Bumpy growls. "Just watch your fucking mouth, you." Despite being one of the whitest men on the planet, he is nicknamed after a famous African-American gangster of the classical period, on account of his tight natural curls, his frankly Negroid nose and lips, and his being, essentially, a gangster.

"A man with no fear", muses Teg. "I respect that, too."

It's not so much that Jase is without fear, though. It's simply that he's been beaten up by Bumpy several times before, and, frankly, it loses its potency after a while, becoming something of a chore. "Yeah. Whatever." He gets to his feet. "Coming, Dai?" But Dai remains seated.

"Working last night, were you?" Teg and Bumpy are amongst the Khans' most extravagant customers, regularly ordering either their tandoori trout or chicken tikka. They realise it would be unwise of them to purchase any meal containing sauces, because they have a good idea of the extra ingredients which Mrs Khan might add, since it is their fault that her only son is now in permanent exile in Bangladesh. "Solid people, Mr and Mrs K. If only their boy hadn't tried to muscle in on our business."

Jase snorts. "And here's me thinking capitalism thrives on competition."

"So naïve." Teg slaps Dai on the back. "So, how we doing, Dai?"

Dai shrugs. "I'm alright."

Teg takes the now-spent joint from Dai's trembling fingers and regards it with a theatrical disdain. "Mari-joo-ahna? Mari-joo-ahna is for hippies and babies. I hates hippies." He pauses, for dramatic effect. "And babies."

"Maybe he fancies something stronger."

Teg turns to Bumpy. "I was coming to that. Didn't you think I was coming to that? Why'd you have to leap in with your fucking size thirteens? You're about as subtle as a fucking sledgehammer!"

If Bumpy is hurt, he conceals it well. There's almost a smile on his unnaturally pale face, as though he and Teg are playing some sado-masochistic game. Which, of course, they are, Jase realises. With Dai playing the role of 'it'. "Dai? Are you coming, or what?"

"No, Jase, I… I just need to talk to the lads about something, mate. Alright?" His eyes are begging Jase to have the strength he himself lacks. Jase turns away and starts to walk down the hill. He loves Dai more than he loves his own life, but he knows that Dai has no such regard for himself. He's tried to drag his friend out of the pit on numerous occasions, only to end up speared on the horns of his indignant self-pity. "When he wants to quit, he'll quit". And anyway, who was there to help Jase, when he was at the bottom of the deep, deep well, reaching out for succour in the darkness? No-one, that was who. Dai was busy cultivating his own addiction, his Mum was, as ever, hogging the role of victim for herself, and as for his dad…

Jase stops dead, halfway towards town. He looks back. Dai has gone, back to Teg and Bumpy's, for a taste of their special medicine. He is conscious of a paradigm-shift in his mind. Simultaneous with his tooth-grinding over Dai, he has been reviewing their conversation. This time, they were actually headed somewhere, he can feel it. Something to do with the desire to make money from music, his inability to write songs. Something to do with professionalism. A tribute band? The bile starts to rise in his duodenum. No, that's not good enough. He thinks about John Peel, about honesty, about integrity. About the need to develop a plan for a project which seamlessly combines cynicism and soulfulness.

And he finds himself thinking once more about his father.

Rewind to the previous New Year's Eve. Party night at the Unaffiliated.

In actuality, every night at the Unaffiliated is something of a party. Alun makes the effort. It's known as the best club night for miles around catering to the mature reveller. There's always something happening, whether it be a comedian, magician, singer, exotic dance troupe (no below-the-waist nudity, thank-you very much), or 'Fifties/'Sixties/'Seventies/'Eighties/'Nineties disco night. And there's always Alun Hopkins, club manager, bingo-caller and regular performer. Of the many Tom Jones acts available throughout the South Wales area, his is generally considered to be, by some distance, the least excruciatingly embarrassing.

New Year's Eve traditionally attracts punters from well beyond the Unaffiliated's customary orbit, as well as pulling in the youth of the town, since the trek into Cardiff is prohibitively expensive, what with inflated venue entry costs, not to mention the taxi situation. Even Jase and Dai have turned up, along with Carol, Dai's big sister, on her first night out since the baby was born. They've entrusted the boy to Jase's mother, who tends to steer clear of the club, what with Alun Hopkins being the bastard who abandoned her when Jase was six, to shack up with a teenage would-be topless model, who later abandoned him for a big-shot from London who actually managed to come through on his promise to get her into the tabloids.

Dai is incoherent, having been on the beers all day, as well as his usual chemical cocktail. Jase spends the evening scouting around for unfamiliar women upon whom to try his particular brand of magic. The first one he approaches looks a bit like "that Jennifer Beals from 'Flashdance'"; the second like "that Mia Farrow in 'Rosemary's Baby'". Neither is especially interested. "Or interesting", grumbles Jase to himself.

There's a disco up until 10.30, at which point the band comes on. Old mates of Alun's, they play hits from the 1960s, and even Jase, who might be characterised as a snob where music is concerned, feels his mood being buoyed by these Beatles, Stones, Kinks and Motown favourites, despite the anodyne nature of their delivery. As midnight strikes, they band plays "Auld Lang Syne", for everyone to sing along, which they all do, even Dai, momentarily risen from his comatose state. Then it's time for Lennon's "Imagine", and a glimpse of a Maoist Utopia. This is followed by the tell-tale organ stabs and guitar licks which signal Tom Jones' "It's Not Unusual", and on bounds Alun, in his black velvet suit, frilly white shirt and ironic (so he tells everyone) medallion. He tears through the song at a more feverish rate than normal, not feeling the need to pace himself since he's not going to be running through his full 90-minute set. There are screams all the way through, which is, actually, not unusual, and Alun allows himself a prematurely self-congratulatory smile as the band hits the final, long chord.

The fat woman does not live locally. She is staying overnight with her sister, and as well as Hogmanay, it is now her 52nd birthday. She has been drinking alco-pops since noon, and her grasp on reality, never all that secure, is steadily slipping. She does not scream with the rest of them during "It's Not Unusual". She is staring, incredulous. Him? Here? But... but how? "Tom..." she mumbles. "You... you came back for me!"

Breasts. Huge, wobbling, porous, white udders. That's all Alun now remembers. One second, he's snapping his fingers along to the band's intro to his second song, "She's A Lady", and the next, the breasts slap into his face, followed by the rest of the birthday girl. They knock him onto his back, and for a full five seconds, he is completely unable to breathe. If you'd have asked him at any previous point about pleasant ways to die, this would have been somewhere near the top of his list. The reality, however, of being suffocated by the unfettered mammaries of a large, drunk, post-menopausal woman, proves to be unenviable. And, as his weeping assailant is dragged off-stage by club security, Alun realises that the shocked audience silence is being broken by an unaccustomed sound – that of his son Jason's hysterical laughter. He also notices that he is unable to move his legs.

The paralysis, attributable to minor contusions of the spinal cord in the upper thoracic region, is short-lived – a matter of minutes. The back pain subsides after a month or so. Even the stage-fright, at least as far as calling the numbers is concerned, has dissipated by Easter. But something dies within Alun, during his sleepless nights in hospital. Not the love of music, or the love of Tom. Not even his desire to sing – he finds himself crooning calmingly to himself even the day after the incident, as he anticipates a bed-bath. But something about the prospect of giving it large in public now makes him want to heave.

"It's simple, Dad", says Jase, bringing a box of sugar-coated brazil-nuts left over from Christmas, on his one and only visit. "You've lost your mojo. It had to happen some time."

Alun has always revelled in his ability to turn heads. Through a fortunate accident of chronology, he contrived to be first in town to adopt the glam rock look in the early 1970s, the punk rock look in the late 1970s, and the New Romantic look in the early 1980s, all involving heavy eye make-up, customised tartan, and being beaten up on a regular basis. It is the last of these incidences which results in Violet, his tentative girlfriend of the moment, gifting him a pity-shag; this resulting in Jason, marriage, and the need to find gainful employment. There thus follows the unhappiest period of Alun's life to date – the pit-head years. When Alun uses the phrase "Thank God for Arthur Scargill", it is a declaration not of righteous radicalism, but of sincere gratitude for the Miners' Strike, the failure of which to salvage the coal industry liberates him, whilst miring the entire region in economic depression. Less than thirty months of service do not entitle him to a great deal of redundancy money, but there is enough to enable him to invest in a frock coat and some business cards. "I'm a singer, Vi – that's all there is to it."

Alun Hopkin's set-list, circa June 1986:

"Gold" (Spandau Ballet)

A punchy one to kick off, start as we mean to go on;

"It's Not Unusual" (Tom Jones)

Moving quickly into a smoochy phase, for the ladies;

"Angel" (Jimi Hendrix – but owing more to the Rod Stewart version)

"Live To Tell" (Madonna)

"Move Closer" (Phyllis Nelson)

And picking up the tempo once more;

"When Doves Cry" (Prince)

"Easy Lover" (Phil Collins/Phillip Bailey)

"Light My Fire" (Doors)

Costume change during Marto's three-minute keyboard solo;

"Light My Fire" - reprise

"If I Was" (Midge Ure)

A bit of a curve-ball, this, but goes down surprisingly well, before we return to solid ground;

"Daughter Of Darkness" (Tom Jones)

Then back to the modern stuff;

"Maneater" (Hall & Oates)

> "True" (Spandau Ballet)

And on to the non-stop finale;

> "Sexual Healing" (Marvin Gaye)

Which is sung to a likely prospect down the front;

> "Addicted To Love" (Robert Palmer)

Delivered with a wink to the men; and finally;

> "I Want To Know What Love Is" (Foreigner)

Sincerity, unity, affirmation. Thank-you very much, you've been a wonderful audience, g'night!

It must be remembered that at this stage in history, Tom Jones is, to the world outside South Wales, Nashville and Las Vegas, largely a name from a kitschy showbiz past. Thus, Alun's early sets lean more heavily on the borderline credible hits of the day – a repertoire which, while it would elicit derisive laughter from audiences of the hip, studenty, indie-rock variety, verges on the dangerously radical as far as clubland is concerned. As does his hair-do, about which no more shall be said.

His collaborator, with a bank of keyboards which would have shamed the wizard Manzarek himself, is Marto Cavanaugh, one of those schoolmates who had disdained Alun's Sweet-esque styling of the glam era, being heavily into Yes, the Floyd and E.L.P. He has spent his post-university years as secondary school music teacher by day, and would-be saviour of progressive rock by night. His decision to stop playing with bands whose songs concern themselves with mythical woodland folk, and take to the clubs with Alun, coincides with the chart success of the weedy, Genesis-influenced Marillion. He takes this as a sign that he has made the right move. The Doors song is his idea, as is the Hendrix and, more surprisingly, perhaps, the Madonna, unless one listens back to the original and notes the intricacy of the synthesizer-dominated backing-track. The rest of the set is down to Alun. Three years on, when Tom has one of his many comeback hits with a version of "Move Closer", Alun is convinced that word of his own arrangement has got back to Jones via the Ponty grapevine. "Me copying him?" He straightens his bootlace tie. "I think you'll find that it's the other way round, squire."

It is perhaps worth nothing that Marto Cavanaugh is Jase's friend Dai's maternal uncle. It is Marto who, when it becomes clear that academia is not destined to be Dai's bag, buys the boy his first rudimentary drum-kit, as a tenth birthday present. It is perhaps not coincidental that Dai starts to go completely off the rails shortly after Marto dies of AIDS-related liver-cancer, five years later. Alun is sceptical: "I knew him from thirteen years old, mun! I spent more time with Marto than anyone! I loved the man! Him dying didn't turn *me* into a fucking junkie!"

Marto is, however, irreplaceable, and even though he took the trouble to commit a number of his arrangements to tape, Alun refuses to go on stage accompanied by an electronic ghost. "I know it looked like we ignored one another when we were up there, but… there was that chemistry. I'll never have that again."

Fortuitously, it is around this time that he is offered the managership of the Unaffiliated. The committee cite his experience as a performer, his knowledge of the entertainment scene in the local area, and his proven ability to put bums on seats. The fact that his lobbying for the post has involved sleeping with three of the committee-members' wives is not mentioned during the interview.

Alun's new status as an employee takes the pressure off, somewhat. He can now afford to be selective when offered gigs, taking, on average, one a fortnight. The "rock" material goes, and he starts to bill himself as a Tom Jones tribute act, since at least then he's sure that whatever combo is available at the various clubs he's engaged at (more usually an old dear at the Yamaha, rather than a full band, with guitars and everything) they're bound to know the songs.

It is at this point that whatever vestigial respect the adolescent Jase might have had for his father, a man whom he generally only ever sees at a distance, dies.

Lucy awakens, beneath the toast-warm duvet. She smiles, and reaches out, but finds herself alone. She opens her eyes, and the clock blinks 7.45 at her. From downstairs comes the sound of the baby's crying. Lucy sighs. It's almost like being a family. She rolls out of bed, and dresses quickly, her clothes having been neatly folded onto the back of the armchair, as part of her seduction ritual. Not that much seduction went on last night. It was fast, rough and satisfying.

Entering the bathroom, she blushes as, glancing in the mirror, she notices the love-bite on her upper lip. Whilst seated on the toilet, she continues to explore it with the tip of her tongue. "I feel cheap. And used." She smiles again.

There is coffee and toast on the breakfast table. Carol is busy burping the baby. "Dai didn't come in last night."

"Yeah. He told you he was meeting up with his mate, at your Mam's."

"Eh?"

"You know. That spotty youth, with the guitar?"

"Oh." Carol frowns. "When was that?"

"You were changing Taylor's nappy. Probably using all your powers of concentration to keep yourself from throwing up on him." Lucy chuckles. "Or is it true that your own baby's poo always smells of lavender?"

"No, it frigging well isn't."

"I only asked." A beaming smile.

"And what are you so cheerful about?"

Lucy shrugs. "Last night. It was… good."

"I've had better." But Carol's smiling now, as well. "You really haven't got the hang of this relationship thing yet, have you? We're past the six month stage, you should be treating me like shit by now."

As Lucy is opening her car door, she notices a denim-clad figure half-limping, half-skipping towards her. "Hey up, Dai. What have you been up to?"

He shrugs. "Just had to see some people. About some stuff." He frowns. "So, are you living here, now?"

"I'm not sure. Are you?"

This is too much of a conundrum for Dai to cope with in his current state. He shakes his head and goes indoors. Lucy waits to hear Carol's shriek of welcome before turning the key in the ignition.

Lucy works as a lab-technician at the town's second-best comprehensive school. As might be expected, her sexual orientation is oft-remarked-upon, but seldom in a vindictive manner. The girls tend towards inquisitiveness, and the boys see hope for redemption in her soft eyes, ladylike manner, and unselfconsciously perky breasts. The severe crew-cut is her only concession to uniformity, and it is this which first prompted Carol to talk to her in the pub one night. Lucy, while not the worldliest woman in existence, could read the signs of bi-curiosity in Carol's attentions. She'd known her by sight ever since moving from Cardiff three years earlier, and seen her with a succession of unpleasant men, concluding, when she eventually turned up pregnant, that that was that. But no – she'd been abandoned. Again. Politically, Lucy objects to the idea of being used by a woman who is "tired of bastard blokes" and wanting to try something new. She'd been going through an epic dry spell, however, and anyway, politics doesn't enter into it when you fancy someone.

The baby is a new experience for Lucy, and not an unpleasing one. Taylor doesn't scream when she holds him, and she feels her heart melt when he smiles at her. Dai is something else entirely. She's known drug-users before, and has occasionally indulged, herself, whilst clubbing. The idea of someone who can barely function on any level without a regular dose is frightening to her, though. But unpredictable though Dai is, he seems harmless, at least as far as other people are concerned. Most of their sporadic conversations have been about music – indeed, there are many more points of convergence here between Lucy and Dai than between Lucy and Carol, whose tastes are strictly high-street. In the early days, she even lends him a couple of CDs, which he promptly sells, or swaps, in order to feed his habit. She quickly realises that the best approach is simply to butt out, although she does tend to slip him a fiver when he begs.

And speak of the devil – as she pauses at the traffic lights, she spots Dai's only discernible friend, the gawky, acne-ridden one, trudging towards the railway station, looking, as always, as though he has something on his mind. Unlike most people round here. She toys with the idea of beeping him, until she remembers that they've never exchanged more than a couple of words. Carol seems to think that Jase has always fancied her, in a "best mate's unattainable older sister" kind of way. But then, Carol's instincts as regards men are, shall we say, unreliable.

Unlike Lucy's, which are a mystery, even to her.

CHAPTER TWO

Alun lives one stop away from Jase on the Valley line; not a long enough journey to enable him to compose his thoughts. In any case, there's no point trying to put together any kind of media-business-type pitch. Alun would laugh him straight back out of the front door, with his skin tingling. As long as the plan remains straight in his mind, Jase feels he'll be able to improvise his way through any awkward questions. Except, of course, the most awkward, this being: "What's the point?"

Alun opens the door in his boxer shorts, Sinatra At The Sands t-shirt, and imitation silk dressing gown. He is visibly taken aback. "Bloody hell! Jason." His eyebrows knit. "Who's dead?"

"No-one. May I?" Alun stands aside, and is amused at the caginess with which Jase looks around the hallway, searching for clues as to the presence of an overnight guest.

"So – do what do I owe this inestimable pleasure?"

Jase smiles. "It's about your mojo."

"What about my mojo?"

"Got anything for breakfast? I'm starving."

As it happens, Alun had a warm loaf of banana bread waiting for him in his machine when he got up that morning. He cuts Jase a couple of slices, as the boy stirs his peppermint tea. "Brilliant things, these." Alun lovingly pats his automatic bread-maker. "Got to grips with yours yet?"

"Not really." Jase knows that Alun knows that his most recent Christmas present to his former wife and child is accumulating dust-mites in the cupboard underneath the sink, along with the wok, the low-fat grill, and the toasted sandwich-maker. The only gift from Alun that Vi employs on a regular basis is the electric carving knife, because of the ease with which she can visualise using it to slice through his chest cavity. "So – seeing anyone at the moment?"

"No-one special. How about you?" Alun suppresses a chuckle. He loves the boy, he truly does, but looks-wise, he definitely takes after his mother.

"Things are a bit quiet at the moment, like. Still – seems as though you aren't doing much better."

"Oh, I don't know. Had a bit of a result on Saturday night." An old friend of a friend, after the bingo. Emphasis on the old. But she was grateful, which always warms the cockles. He brings Jase his bread, and sits across the kitchen table from him. "So – what's this proposition you've got for me?"

"Well, Dad… it's like… I…" Jase pulls himself together. "I want you to be the singer in my new band."

There's a tumbleweed moment, as Alun takes this in, too calmly for comfort. "Okay, Jason – run that by me again?"

"I'm starting a band. And I want you to be the lead singer."

Jase was expecting laughter, incredulity, ridicule. The unmistakable birth of a tear in the corner of the old man's eye comes as a shock. "Erm… are you taking the piss?"

Jase chokes back his reflexive, sarcastic reply. "Listen, Dad – what was the first record you ever got me?"

"The Muppets."

"The first proper record."

"Dean Martin, 'This Time I'm Swingin''"

"The first proper record that I actually listened to more than once."

"Everly Brothers. 'Songs Our Daddy Taught Us.'"

"The first proper record that made me believe we might actually have something in common."

Alun has to think about this one. "'Scott Walker Sings Jacques Brel'!" He can tell from Jase's expression that things are not going by the book. "I've bought you lots of records, son.

"Yeah, but…" Jase takes a deep breath. "The first album where you gave the impression that you might actually know something about me."

Ah. This must have something to do with that guitar of his. A gift from his good old Dad. Therefore: "Robert Johnson. 'King of the Delta Blues.'"

"At last!"

Without prompting, Alun starts to sing, dragging the pit of his soul. About believing, believing that his time ain't long.

Jase snaps his fingers. "See! That's exactly what I'm talking about!"

"W-what?"

"You're a good singer, Dad. And I'm a good guitar-player. And I really think we can do this. I mean, I know how the business works, I mean, I've been watching you for years, and I read the music papers, and I listen to the radio, and I talk to people, and I followed Dai's whole experience, and I know how things are. I mean… I've never been in a band, which is something I really should have done, because I know you'd have supported me, I know you'd have come and see me play, like I used to come and see you. And I know you're old… well, no, obviously, you're not old, 46 isn't old, not these days. I mean, if we were talking about some indie or dance or electro band trying to be hip, trying to be cool, yeah, it's old. But if we're talking the blues, it's no age at all.

And you've got the voice, you've been through the shit, you've worked down a coal-mine, for fuck's sake! And you've put other people though shit, and that's part of it, too. And you know how to work a crowd without looking like you're working the crowd. And you know music, and you love music, it's part of you, like it's part of me. And I've got to do something, or I'll bust, man, swear to God, my fuckin' head'll explode. 'Cause that's what the whole drugs things was about, it was frustration and having no hope and having no confidence. It was about not having a plan. But now, I've got a plan."

This is Jase's highest ever word-count in a non-shouted conversation with his father. Alun is moved. "Let me get this straight, son – you're starting a blues band, and you want me to be the lead singer."

"Right. But… I've got conditions, though."

"Conditions? Hold your horses, there, son." He finds Jase's resolve both puzzling and impressive. "I think you're forgetting. I've retired."

"No. You just lost it. Because you were doing this Tom Jones shit. You were being…" A stray phrase from his reading of Camus in A-Level French swims into view. "You were being existentially inauthentic. You weren't being you."

"I've got more in common with Tom Jones than I do with… this may have escaped your attention, Jason, but we are not the disenfranchised grandchildren of African slaves in the Southern States of America."

Jase's nostrils flare. "Are you honestly telling me that you don't have the blues in your soul."

"Everybody's got the blues in their soul. It's called being a human being."

"Yes!" Jase bangs the table, causing Alun to jump. "And not being able to express it in a healthy way is what fucks us up. Except… you've got a gift.

And I think I have as well. We can use it to make people feel better. And… you know, maybe make some money."

Alun guffaws. "Money?"

"Not silly money. I mean… gigging money. Professional musician money. Like you've been doing all these years."

"Jason… I'm not a rich man."

"You've got a house, a car, a pension plan. You saw me alright, financially. Plus however many other kids you've got out there." This is a subject the contemplation of which generally makes Jase shudder, but right now he has a point to make. "I don't want to be rich. Rich people are arseholes. I want to make a living, that's all."

There is a long silence, while Alun attempts to order his thoughts. They are dominated by the oddness of this new, dynamic Jason. "So… what are these conditions, then?"

"Number one – my band, my rules."

Alun has anticipated this one, though not the vehemence with which the notion is expressed. "Fair enough."

"I mean, I'll need your advice, and the benefit of all your experience and that, and of course I'll listen to all sensible suggestions, but… it's my band."

"I said, fair enough."

"Oh. Right."

"Next condition?"

A twitch of the eye, then: "Dai's on drums."

Alun pretends to almost fall off his chair. "Dai Williams? Are you serious? That junkie waster?"

"He's my best friend. And he's a fucking good drummer."

There then follows an extended discussion of Dai's merits as a percussionist balanced against his demerits as a human being, central to which is Alun's breathless recitation of an extensive catalogue of petty thefts, mishaps and let-downs.

"I hear what you're saying, Dad." But Jase is immovable. "This is probably the only way to save his life. You remember what happened with his uncle."

This is hitting below the belt. "Marto died."

"Yeah, but... you know." Marto was gigging with Alun up until a fortnight before he passed, even though he'd been forced to take several months sick-leave from school. No-one who witnessed his work ethic in action could have imagined that the keyboard maestro was terminally ill. "Music kept him going for ages."

"Dai is not fit to lace Marto Cavanaugh's shoes."

"Bottom line, Dad – you've seen him play drums. Is he good, or what?"

Alun shrugs. "He can play drums. So what? Hitler could paint."

"I can handle Dai, alright. And whose band is it?"

"It isn't anybody's band, yet."

"Look... Dad... it wouldn't be hard to find another singer. Not round here. I could throw a stone and hit half a dozen musical theatre queens. I just thought it might be nice..." His voice cracks, only half-intentional. "You know, like, being a family, for once."

Alun flinches. "Emotional blackmail, is it? So what's the next condition?"

"The next condition is – my band, my rules."

"That's the same as the first condition."

"And the fourth, fifth and sixth." Jase leans forward, fixing his father with a steel-tipped gaze. "I'm taking this seriously."

"Yeah, well…" Alun is the first to look away. "I'll think about it."

"Damn right you'll think about it", barks Jase, forceful. Undermining the effect by asking for another cup of peppermint tea, please. "And could you do me a slice of toast?"

Dai awakens around five in the afternoon, every muscle aching, as per usual. His recollection of what occurred with Teg and Bumpy that morning is mercifully vague. He remembers being tied to something, he remembers something untoward occurring in his rectal area. He runs his tongue around his mouth to see if he can call up a sense memory of anything unwelcome having been crammed into it. No. Good.

He lies still for a while, attempting to gauge the state of his bloodstream. Hm. It's been better, but it's also been considerably worse. He reaches underneath the mattress, and pulls out his biscuit-tin. His fingers are steady as he opens it, which is a good sign. He's delighted to discover that Teg has seen him right; the good stuff is there, in bounteous proportions. This so cheers him that he feels able to roll out of bed and leave his bedroom without sorting himself out.

"Evening, lezzers!" Carol and Lucy look up from their meal as he enters the dining-room, apprehension in both sets of eyes. "What you eating?"

It's a salmon stew, and there's plenty left in the kitchen. On his way back to the table, the telephone rings. He instinctively checks the caller display, a feature which is invaluable to Carol, given her history with unsound men. It's Jase.

"Hey, Dai, mate. Remember that thing we were talking about this morning?"

"Seriously, bro, what are the chances of that?"

Dai listens as Jase outlines his plan. "So, how does it sound?"

"Yeah, yeah. I like it." He lowers his voice, conscious of an audience. "Erm… thanks for thinking of me."

"You're the best drummer I know. Well, you're the only drummer I know."

"Bastard."

Dai is smiling as he takes his place at the dinner-table.

"So, what was that all about?" Carol is relieved to be able to keep it light, for once, in conversation with her baby brother.

"It's Jase. He's finally getting his band together."

"Oh." Lucy is surprised. "You mean he's never done it before?"

"He's shy," offers Carol, patronising.

"No, I just thought… what kind of band?"

"Blues. Nice stew." He pauses, with the spoon halfway to his mouth. "I'm trying to think of a joke about lesbians being bound to be good at making recipes with fish in them, but I'm not quite getting there."

"No, it's just…" Lucy has noticed how eagerly Dai looks forward to his jam sessions with Jase, and how calm he appears to be afterwards, irrespective of whether or not he's had his other kind of fix. "I thought you'd both done the band thing."

"Nah. Just me. I'm the together one, see." He winks at her. "Go figure."

While weekends are, naturally enough, the most frantic time for deliveries from Khan's Curry Kitchen, mid-weeks are generally no picnic either.

They make it a policy not to deliver outside a five-mile radius, however, Samira being sensitive about the effect of reheating, "especially in one of those accursed microwaves", on her unique blend of spices ("The secret ingredient is love", she once told a trade magazine journalist; although it is actually Jamaican nutmeg soaked in lime-juice). Nor do they serve certain areas after 9pm, due to the likelihood of the orders having being placed with the express intention of ultra-violence being visited upon the driver. Thus, Jase has it relatively easy, and spends a lot of time chatting with Mo, mostly about politics (they cordially accuse one another of being reactionary re America's War On Terror) and music. Jase gives Mo tips on vintage soul artists with whom he might be unfamiliar (a notable discovery being James Carr, whom Jase first heard via John Peel), while Mo has got his son to send over a number of fascinating CDs by Bangladeshi heavy metal bands, which Jase finds generally too polished, but it's the thought that counts.

Tonight, Mo discerns Jase's restlessness. "So you're really going to do it this time, uh?"

In the year or so since Jase spotted the advert in the Khans' window and found himself asking for the job even before realising what he was playing at, Jase has often spoken of his need to remove his finger from his fundament and make his guitar-playing pay. "It's now or never, Mo."

Mo was working last New Year's Eve, but Alun's accident was the talk of the area for several weeks. "But what about your Dad's stage-fright?"

"It wasn't stage-fright. It was a sudden realisation that he was in the wrong place, at the wrong time, being the wrong person." Whilst refining his plan throughout the day, Jase has come up with a theory. "All the great singers are blues singers, Mo. Billie Holiday, Pavarotti, Nusrat Fateh Ali Khan, Johnny Rotten, Bob Marley... listen to a Bach violin sonata, or a Chopin piano prelude, or any Beethoven... Jewish klezmer... Portuguese fado... Senegalese kora stuff... it's all about loss, longing, loneliness... the very stuff of the human spirit. The very thing that makes music... central to the existence of any civilised being. It's all the blues!"

Mo recollects that when John Lee Hooker was a guest on "Desert Island Discs" on Radio Four, and asked to choose a book which would, ideally, accompany him, were he cast away in the midst of the unforgiving ocean, the legendary bluesman claimed that he wasn't so hot on literature, and wondered if he might, instead, be allowed a magazine with pictures of pretty ladies in it. He and Jase laugh so mischievously that Samira pops her head out from the kitchen to enquire as to what filth it is they're talking.

Jase knocks off at 10.30, and as he walks through the streets, self-consciously toting his guitar-case, he wonders if this is the last time he'll read the message "You Are A Fake!" in the eyes of passers-by.

CHAPTER THREE

Dai is the first to arrive at the rehearsal venue. It is the usual place, his mother's garage, but in his case, prompt attendance doesn't necessarily follow from this. As Jase walks in, Dai is keeping a steady Chicago-house-style beat. For the zillionth time, Jase marvels at his space-age co-ordination and metronomic precision. Dai nods at Jase, but continues to play, happy to be lost in that parallel universe where rhythm is king. Jase unpacks his guitar, and plugs in, but does not, as is the routine, immediately surf Dai's wave. He simply stands there, fingers caressing his axe, waiting.

When Dai stops playing, he makes as if to go and build their customary spliff, but Jase raises a hand. "No – we'll start as we mean to go on. 'Yer Blues'. Beatles."

Dai is a little stung by Jase's abruptness, and gives a semi-ironic salute before settling back on his seat, and going into waltz time. Jase gives him a few bars, before weakly essaying the vocal, following this with the crashing guitar line, continuing in this call-response mode, until the end of the verse, at which point Dai joins in on the line about the girl knowing the reason why, equally feeble. Jase moves onto the second verse, giving the vox a little more welly, but this time, Dai fails to join in on the chorus, and Jase himself decides to play the remainder of the vocal lines on guitar, calling and responding to himself with some fluency.

It is while they are in mid-flow that Alun, who has been listening outside, lifts up the garage door and ducks underneath. Without betraying the fact that he has spotted him, Jase does an especially flashy minor scale arpeggio at triple speed, before looking up, and ostentatiously signalling for Dai to halt. "Alright, Dad?"

"Jason. David."

"Wotcha, Mr Hopkins."

Alun looks around the garage. Paint tins, rusted tools, old music magazines. The smell of damp. "Ooh. Swish!"

"We could always practise round at yours, Mr H."

Alun scowls at Dai. "You can string a sentence together, can you? Is that a good sign, or a bad sign?"

"I'm sorry?"

"Does it mean that you've taken heroin, or that you haven't taken heroin?"

"That's for me to know and you to find out." With a 'ba-dum-tsh' on his kit.

"I'm serious. I don't work with druggies."

"Get real, Dad. All your years round the clubs, you never once had a sniff of white powder?"

Alun shrugs. "Maybe once or twice. Years ago." He winces at an unwelcome memory. "It had a deleterious effect on my sexual performance."

Dai groans, while Jase shudders and pretends to vomit. "Too much information, Dad. Look – Dai's job is to play the drums. That's all that need concern you, right?"

Alun gives Dai a hard Paddington stare. Dai responds with a Joker grin. Alun rolls his eyes, and opens his briefcase. He has brought his microphone. "I'll plug this into your amp for now, shall I, son?"

It's back to first positions for "Yer Blues", once more, Alun being well *au fait* with the lyrics. Six minutes into Jase's guitar solo, Alun signals for Dai to lay down his sticks.

"Son – alright, I get the picture. You can play the guitar. And it's your band, your rules. But are you familiar with the phrase 'less is more'?"

"Dad – this is the first song in our first rehearsal. I'm just showing you what I can do."

"Son – I have faith in you." Alun rests a hand on the boy's shoulder. "And you should have faith in the songs."

Jase dusts the hand from his person. "Are you familiar with the phrase 'pompous git'?!"

"All I'm saying is that grandstanding is going to get in the way of the fucking material!"

There follows a heated debate taking in such subjects as the definition of "grandstanding", the extent to which a vocalist of mature years might be more prone to it than his introvert son, the ownership of the band, the extent to which said band will exist should the putative singer decide to say "fuck it" and go home, and the need (or otherwise) for the junkie drummer to stick his bastard oar in. The conversation appears to be approaching a decisive climax when the garage door swings up, and a newcomer stands blinking in the low light. The individual is wearing a conservative grey suit, and carrying a hard guitar-case.

"Alright, guys?"

Dai slaps his forehead. "Oh yeah – my sister's girlfriend was wondering if she could audition to play bass in our band. Completely slipped my mind."

While Lucy and Dai are collecting her amp from the back seat of her Citroen, Alun and Jase consider the situation, *sotto voce.*

"I mean, what were you going to do about a bass-player, anyway?"

"Well, if worst came to the worst…" Jase shrugs. "I mean, White Stripes, Black Keys - they don't have bass-players."

"In my experience, women in bands… they're… they're a distraction."

"Dad – she likes girls. None of us have got a chance with her, anyway."

"That's not what I meant."

"Yes it is."

"You could always advertise."

"No. Look at the best bands – the Beatles, Stones, U2, Smiths, Oasis – they didn't advertise. They came together naturally. Organically. As mates."

"But we aren't mates. I've scarcely laid eyes on her before."

"I've met her a couple of times." Awkward half-conversations at Carol's, whilst waiting for Dai to get his shit together, prior to a boys' night out. Once in Spiller's Records in Cardiff, when they said hello; then five minutes later in HMV Records in Cardiff, when they ignored one another. "She's alright."

"For a carpet-muncher."

"And here's me thinking you were a liberal."

"I'm all for gay rights, son. I just don't trust lesbians." Another dark memory from clubland re-ignites his nervous tic. "Or transvestites."

Jase frowns. "They aren't the same thing, Dad."

"I know. Just thank the Good Lord you didn't have to find out the hard way."

Jase is still inwardly wrestling with the idea of pursuing this, when Dai and Lucy return, and they set up.

"Alright, darling. Show us what you can do."

Jase glares at Alun, who bows apologetically, and takes a step back. Jase clears his throat. "Okay, Lucy. Show us… w-what you can do."

What Lucy can do is deliver an achingly heartfelt version of the delicate Jimi Hendrix ballad "Little Wing", essaying both melody line and bass part, with added baroque curlicues. The boys look at one another.

"Yeah, well that was alright, I suppose."

Smiling a fake-modest smile, Lucy segues into the disco bass-line from the Rolling Stones "Miss You", and has to leap out of the way as Dai stampedes back to his drum-kit. Jase and Alun step backwards, arms folded, as the freshly minted rhythm section consummate their relationship.

"So what do you reckon?"

"She's good." Alun does his best James Finlayson double-take. "But what are you asking me for? It's your band."

"I wasn't asking you about Lucy. I mean, Lucy was in the band as soon as she came in the room. Her being able to play is just a bonus."

"Eh? How do you work that out?"

"She fits with the design concept. We're all misfits. You included. So? Are you in?"

The first song they do as a band is "Yer Blues". The second is "Heartbreak Hotel", a version owing more to the John Cale version than Elvis, which comes together far more quickly than any of them have the right to expect. A little breathless, they adjourn to Dai's mother's kitchen for their first business meeting, at which the first issue up for democratic consideration is the band's name.

"Ofnadwy Bluesville," announces Jase.

"What?" A trio of perplexed expressions.

"We are Ofnadwy Bluesville."

 "What the fuck is that about?" wonders Alun.

"'Ofnadwy' means… 'awful', doesn't it?" Lucy has neglected her Welsh since attaining a bare pass at G.C.S.E.

"It's a sincere tribute to our home town."

"But Lucy's from Cardiff."

"And you forget – I was born in Neath," contributes Alun. "Plus, technically, I no longer live in this town."

"Erm – whose band is this?"

Lucy smiles. "That's sounding more and more like a catchphrase."

The second item on the agenda is material. Jase reads out his list of songs:

"Yer Blues", the Beatles, and Elv's "Heartbreak Hotel", already on the way to being nailed.

"Old Man Trouble" – the first track from Otis Redding's classic "Otis Blue" album, at which everyone grunts approval.

"Spooky", with which Lucy is unfamiliar until Alun gives her a verse and chorus.

"Don't Let Me Be Misunderstood", at which Alun punches the air – one of his many theme songs. "Let's face it", says Jase, "It's everybody's theme song."

"Ain't No Love In The Heart Of The City", "I Heard It Through The Grapevine", and "Ain't No Sunshine", which get everyone nodding.

And finally, Jase ventures into '70s rock for Marc Bolan's tender "Life's A Gas", and "No Matter What", by Swansea's Badfinger.

"Why do I get the feeling that you're quite used to making lists of ten?" Lucy jumps. "Oh, I'm sorry, did I say that out loud?"

"Of course, we'll need to work together to come up with arrangements which suit everybody. And, naturally, if you can think of songs you'd like to have a go at…"

"Your generosity knows no bounds", admits Alun.

"Although there are a few ground rules. Like… no more than one song by the same person. We are not a tribute band. No more than a couple of Motowns, no more than a couple of clichéd blues standards. And nothing too cool, or cutesy-clever, like a Coldplay song, or anything by Blur. In fact…" Jase is thinking as he goes, "no cover versions more recent than 1990."

"'Blues In The Night'" offers Alun, immediately bouncing back to the 1940s, initially with sarcastic intent, but hushing his mouth when it is met with approval.

"What about 'Anyone Who Had A Heart'?", suggests Lucy.

"Dusty Springfield?" Alun snorts. "Do you actually know any songs not sung by lesbians?"

"Do you actually know any songs not sung by geriatrics?", counters Lucy, struggling to retain her good humour. And succeeding when she sees that he has no comeback.

"'Touch The Hem Of His Garment.'" Everyone turns to look at Dai. "Gospel song. Sam Cooke. About the Bible. You know. This woman touches the hem of Jesus's robe, and she's cured, like."

Alun states the obvious. "I, er, never figured you for the religious type, Dai."

"It's a nice song. And I like the idea of people being cured of things."

"Fair enough."

"Elvis Costello – 'Almost Blue'." This is Lucy again. "I mean, I know he did 'Don't Let Me Be Misunderstood' as well, but that doesn't count as two Costellos, does it?"

Jase adds it to his list. And, just as they are about to move on to the next item.

"Hold on a moment – we've got to do a Woodward." Alun often refers to Tom Jones' oeuvre by the singer's original name, misguidedly affecting an unearned and unearnable intimacy.

"I thought you'd retired from the cheese business, Dad." Jase, with a heavy heart, has been expecting this. "I mean, I've got nothing against menopausal women, personally, but I was hoping we could go for a more… musically sophisticated audience."

Lucy and Dai stifle their giggles. Alun shakes his head, pitying them in their ignorance, and sings a verse and chorus of "It Looks Like I'm Never Going To Fall In Love Again", accompanied only by the humming of the refrigerator.

Dai discovers an obstruction in his throat, and Lucy finds herself wiping an itch from the corner of her eye. Jase sniffs. "Yeah, well, maybe we can do something with that."

Item three is the next rehearsal, and they agree on two extended sessions, taking up most of the following weekend.

"Any other business?"

"Erm…" Lucy is hesitant. "Well… if we're a proper band now… shouldn't we do a… a group hug, or a huddle, or something like that?"

Alun rolls his eyes, in response to which, Jase pretends to take the idea seriously, in response to which Dai starts to chase him around the room, lips pursed, arms akimbo. Eventually, they compromise with a round-robin of manly handshakes, and the meeting is adjourned.

Jase helps Lucy to put her amp in her car, and she offers him a ride home. Jase accepts, Alun having taken his leave pretty sharpish when the prospect of heavy lifting presented itself.

"I'd never heard your father sing before." Lucy breaks the silence, with the journey almost concluded. "I knew he was supposed to be good but… well, the phrase 'pleasantly surprised' comes to mind."

"He's a better-than-average club singer." Jase smiles grimly. "He's like me. All style, no originality. How long have you been playing?"

"Nine, ten years. Since the sixth form. I was…" She pauses, and sighs. "There was this girl I liked, and she had a band, and she said I could join if I got a bass."

"And what happened?"

"Well, we became world-famous teenage rock stars, and got married, and lived happily ever after."

"Sorry. Intruding."

"She went away to university. I didn't. End of story."

"Oh." Another long silence. "Too thick for uni, eh?"

"It's not quite as simple as that." And before she quite knows what she's doing, the whole story is spilling out, about being thrown out by her church-going parents at fifteen because of "the whole being queer thing", and the bizarreness of life in a care home disrupting her studies, and clinging to the first job she could get after school, and being shocked that she was competent at something, and deciding to stick with that line of work because it didn't make the kind of demands that would negatively affect her social life, but actually spending most of her evenings fiddling with her bass, because she's not very good at figuring out the dating business.

"Yeah. You and me both." By this time, they are parked outside Jase's mother's house. "Still. At least you've got Carol, now."

"Yeah. Till she decides she fancies… you know." She blushes in the darkness. "A bit of dick."

"So, you've never… you know… with a bloke, like?"

"A few times. Not quite my thing. There was this…" She hesitates, but it is too late. "That thing about maybe lesbians not liking it because they haven't met a bloke who can do it right. I… there was this bloke at my last job… he was supposed to be this real stud… so I had a go."

"And?"

"Well, it wasn't dreadful, or anything. But I was still a lesbian." She is about to ask polite, reciprocal questions about his life, but he forestalls them.

"So – the band. Do you reckon it's a goer?"

"Ofnadwy Bluesville." She savours the words like a fine wine. "I don't see why not. As long as you can keep us in line."

"Well, it's not really a question of being able to." He opens the car door. "It's a question of not having any choice in the matter. See you."

"He's what?!" This is Violet, Jase's mother, being as animated as she can manage these days, as she watches him eat the lunch she's prepared for him.

"The lead singer." Matter-of-factly. "Of my band."

"You... but you can't!"

"It'll be alright, Mum"

"You can't! Not after what he did to us!"

Jase rests his free hand on hers, which is trembling. "Mum – what he did to you and what he did to me are two different things. I'm taking steps to deal with my problems with the man. I can't deal with yours."

He resumes eating his broken omelette with burnt-on-the outside-frozen on-the-inside oven chips. He is better at cooking than her, due to all the time he had to look after himself while he was growing up, because she was in bed with her nerves. Violet has been better able to cope these past few years; she seemed to draw strength from Jase's recovery from drug-addiction, this coinciding with the relaxing slide into middle age. She's even broken her duck man-wise, having taken up with old Jefferson, the taxi-driver, whom Jase finds physically repellent, but he seems to treat her with respect, which is the most important thing. Jase had hoped that she might finally be ceasing to define herself solely in terms of Alun's abandonment of her. Clearly, though, there is still some way to go.

"I don't care about me. I just don't want him hurting you any more. I don't want him letting you down again."

"If he lets me down, I'll sack him." Jase feels the heat of her puzzled gaze. "It's my band, you see, Mum. I'm running things. It's my way, or the highway. My road, or the road to Palookaville. My path, or the path to destruction. The Jason Hopkins Motorway, or Little Al's cul-de-sac."

"But..." Vi remains unconvinced. "Having to cope with your dad, on top of David!"

"I can handle Dai." Having had to handle his mother, and her tranquilliser problem for as long as he could remember. Before he himself succumbed. "I'm a stronger person than you think I am."

"Oh. Well." She has no grounds on which to dispute this. "So – what's that Lucy girl like?"

"She seems pleasant enough. Good bass-player."

"She's quite pretty."

Jase laughs. "She's a lesbian, Mum. And even if she wasn't, if I fancied her and told her so, she'd probably pretend she was."

"Still." Vi is conscious that Jase's repeated failures with young ladies may have contributed to his resorting to heroin. And that, perhaps, her hatred of his father may have soured the idea of relationships for him altogether. "Playing with this band, you might meet someone nice."

"Yes, Mum." Jase removes a fragment of eggshell from a gap in his teeth. "Blues revival bands always attract the choicest groupies."

But this gets Vi thinking about Alun's misbehaviour once more, and the conversation degenerates.

CHAPTER FOUR

Snapshots from the day preceding Ofnadwy Bluesville's first extended rehearsal session:

14.43. Dai and Jase, sitting, wordless and cosy in the pub, second pint of the day. Dai is drumming on the table with his index fingers, eyes closed. Jase is scribbling once more on the tattered sheet of A4, crossing out numbers next to song-titles, as he attempts to fashion the perfect sequence.

16.18. Alun, having showered and perfumed himself in preparation for his evening at the Unaffiliated, doing the moves to "It's Not Unusual" in front of his full-length wardrobe mirror. He is wearing only his underpants (one size too small, which he has been told is flattering), and miming into his microphone.

03.04. Lucy, perched on the corner of the bed, running through minor-key scales, at increasing speeds, on her unplugged bass. Carol, who has quietly awakened, reaches out to stroke her naked back.

Saturday morning, 09.40. Dai's mother's garage, all band-members are present, if not exactly correct, Friday night having been a big one for all, except Jase, who spent most of his time at the wheel working on song-treatments.

They run through "Yer Blues" and "Heartbreak Hotel" again, to confirm that the progress made last time wasn't a fluke. "Ain't No Sunshine" and "Spooky" are the next to be tackled, and progress is even more straightforward, partly down to the fact that they don't stray too far from the familiar arrangements. Lucy has also taken the trouble to go through the song-list and download the lyrics from the Internet, thus curbing Alun's tendency to extemporise.

"Old Man Trouble" follows, Jase having spent some time working on the guitar intro, incorporating some potentially amusing silences. Progressing into the song, however, it becomes clear that Lucy has little to do, and that the horn flourishes of the original are sorely missed. Lucy suggests that she take on the responsibility of the introduction, as well as the bulk of the extant guitar part, and they try once more, with Jase's bluesy licks replacing the original's four-man brass section.

"Yeah, that worked," concedes Jase.

Lucy detects that he feels slightly stung, and keeps quiet as they work on "No Matter What", which is surprisingly tricky, the problem being the need to avoid its sounding like a straight cover-version. Alun compensates by injecting an extra growl into his vocal, and Jase resorts to letting the band run through it without him for a while, then weaving in simple guitar lines, culminating in a lengthy solo near the end.

"Can we have a vote?", wonders Alun, as they take a tea-break.

"Since when was this a democracy?" Jase is worried.

"I propose an upper limit of one minute for guitar solos. Any takers?" Alun raises a hand in support of his own proposition.

Tentatively, Lucy follows suit. "Nothing personal, Jase. I'm just thinking about the songs."

All eyes turn to Dai. "I abstain."

"On what grounds?"

"Conflict of interest. On the one hand, Jase is my mate. On the other, I agree with you two. It's a mind-fucker, dudes."

Jase is surprised that he does not feel more slighted. A lack of respect for his guitar-playing, it appears that he can handle. If they didn't care about the purity of the Ofnadwy Bluesville concept, that would hurt. "Fair enough."

Alun is a little taken aback at Jase's equanimity. "I… I mean, it might be… you know, appropriate for a couple of tunes… towards the end of the set, like."

"Thanks. I'll think about it."

As it happens, the next tune they go for is "Ain't No Love In The Heart Of The City", which provides plenty of scope for modestly showy guitar work. In contrast, "Don't Let Me Be Misunderstood" is sluggish, and they abandon their third attempt half way through. Jase sets up the tape-recorder, and they run through their first seven songs without a break.

The mood prior to playback is tetchy, as they all check their watches. Despite the muddy reproduction, and the occasional dubious note, however, the results are heartening; the intent shines through, their respect for the material being plain to see, and there is more than a modicum of soul evident.

"Damn, but I'm good!" Alun is only half joking.

"We're all good." Jase nods. "No, seriously. Good work, guys."

"Well, I think the bandleader should take some of the blame."

Jase is disoriented by this unaccustomed plaudit from his father, not to mention the affectionate punches on the arm from the other two. "Well, we've still got a shitload of work to do. There's those other songs. Plus, we've got to get slicker."

Alun licks a finger and smoothes his eyebrows. "If I was any slicker than I am right now, I'd be a hazard to shipping."

"Anyway, we don't want to get rid of all the rough edges, do we?" Lucy is rather more cheerful than she sounds. "I mean, it's the blues, innit?"

All too soon, the meeting has broken up. Dai rushes off to take care of his bloodstream, Alun has business to take care of at the Unaffiliated, and Lucy is obligated to go on a shopping-trip with Carol. While Jase does not exactly float home on a cushion of air, those passers-by who know him by sight detect an unusual bounce in his step, and the guitar case is wielded with more assurance than before.

Back home, a meal of burnt pork chops with lumpy mashed potatoes is waiting for him. "Well? How did it go?"

Aware that his mother is hoping for bad news, Jase lets her down gently. "Yeah. Not bad, actually."

That evening at the Khans', he is free to fizz with enthusiasm, as he attacks his real dinner, a lamb vindaloo with extra mushrooms. "And Dai was so disciplined. I mean, he's always been a wild man, I mean, that's why he got that big gig, they were a wild band. But today, he just sat there, he just slotted in, he was really feeling it, I could tell."

"David was always such a good-looking boy. It's just such a pity that he…" Samira breaks off, unable to go deep into Dai's friendship with their exiled son, who was one of his earliest suppliers. "It will be good if this enterprise can… give him something healthy to focus on."

Jase makes a mental note of another song title: "I Don't Believe In Miracles."

It should go without saying that Sunday's rehearsal is a complete bollix, at least to begin with. Out of all of them, it is teacher's pet Lucy who is late, having treated Carol to a night out in Cardiff, from which they didn't get back until three in the morning. By the time she turns up, they have tried and abandoned "Don't Let Me Be Misunderstood" again, and attempted "I Don't Believe In Miracles", although Alun can get nowhere near the high notes, which irritates him. Lucy is punished for her tardiness by being ordered to show them her arrangement for "Anyone Who Had A Heart". Alun makes fun of her voice, which is fairly weak to begin with, but enfeebled further by her desire for the veins throbbing in her head not to rupture completely.

An hour in, they have accomplished nothing. Jase plays the tape of Saturday's proceedings once more, which lightens the mood. They run through "Ain't No Love In The Heart Of The City", for no reason other than Jase's hunch that it will cheer them all up. It succeeds, and "Life's a Gas", "I Heard It Through The Grapevine", and Alun's "It Looks Like I'm Never Going To Fall In Love Again" are sorted out in fairly short order.

During the tea-break, Jase starts to take them through their options. "Okay, so we've got ten songs down – not bad, considering."

"Considering we've suddenly turned shit, you mean?" This time, Alun's performance of the Woodward, though perfectly fine, has brought the mood down, and he knows it.

"Which of these other songs are we definitely doing?"

Lucy opens her mouth to suggest having another crack at her Bacharach and David, then suddenly claps a hand over it, and rushes upstairs to be spectacularly sick into Dai's mother's lavatory. As she is disgorging last night's Chinese into the off-white bowl, the onomatopoeic appropriateness of the Antipodean word "chunder" comes to mind, and when she returns to the sofa, she has had a change of heart. "Crowded House – 'Don't Dream It's Over'."

When they return to the garage, this is the first song they try, and it works. Next up is "Touch The Hem Of His Garment", Dai's chosen gospel classic, which Alun especially likes because there is no room for a guitar solo. Similarly, he decides that for the bulk of "Blues In The Night", only Lucy and

Dai will be required, although he allows Jase an extended instrumental break before the final verse.

"Thirteen songs", muses Dai. "We can't stop there, man. Bad ju-ju."

There is a collective sigh, as "Don't Let Me Be Misunderstood" looms once more. As they are approaching the second chorus of their umpteenth plod through the piece, Dai stops playing. When the others turn to look at him in puzzlement, he starts up a steady funk beat. Jase watches his father's eyes narrow, as he seems about to completely lose patience. Alun takes a deep breath, as if to scream at Dai. What comes out, though, is the first verse, delivered with some venom. By the time they reach the chorus, they are both smiling, although Jase and Lucy remain at a loss. They continue to be bemused spectators, until the end of the middle eight, when Alun drops his head, and points at each of them simultaneously, in a crucifixion pose. Acting purely on instinct, Jase plays a jazzy, fluid line and then breaks off; Lucy then takes up the reins; Jase follows her – and before they know it, they are indulging in a 1970s-style guitar duel, first swapping extravagant licks, then coming together to play the melody in unison, then lapsing into free-form absurdity, before Dai brings matters to a close with a random, arrhythmic solo. The silence which ensues is heavy with befuddlement. Lucy is the first to speak.

"Erm… I kind of enjoyed that."

Jase glances over and sees that the tape machine has been running the whole time. "Yeah. Maybe we can do something with it."

"Like forget it ever happened?" But Alun is smiling.

"Er – can I go and have my dinner, now?" Dai is not the only one who looks drained. It is clearly time to call it a day.

Jase awakens twice in the middle of the following night.

The first time is when he hears moaning coming from his mother's bedroom, and he is about to get up to see if she is in need of medical assistance when he recalls that her friend Jefferson is staying the night. Groaning, he covers his head with the pillow.

The second time is in response to a nightmare, the precise details of which evaporate in an instant. Something to do with the band. Like they've got a gig that very night, in front of sixty-five thousand people at the Millennium Stadium, and they've only got one song ready, and none of them can remember what it's called. He gets up and goes to the toilet, then, on returning to his room, puts on the tapes of the weekend's sessions.

Yes, it's messy; yes, it's ragged; and his guitar-playing doesn't have quite as much panache as it does in his head; and Alun does sound somewhat more like a self-satisfied clubland entertainer than a grizzled denizen of the Mississippi Delta. But Dai's drumming is shit-hot, and Lucy's bass-playing is richly, effortlessly contrapuntal. And, let's face it, they've taught themselves fourteen songs in two days. Not bad going for a bunch of losers.

"Who are you calling a loser?" This is early on Tuesday evening, when Jase pops round to Lucy's, on the way to the Curry Kitchen. "I'm offended."

Lucy's tiny house is in the middle of a crumbling terraced block, which the estate agent described as possessing a quasi-rustic charm, largely because of its proximity to a wan excuse for a field, which used to be a steelworks. Still, Lucy isn't fussy about this kind of thing. She needed to get out of Cardiff, she wanted a home of her own, and it was affordable, even on her limited income. When Jase was growing up, this area was full of old people, but now it's a bit of a ghetto for young couples and singles grown weary of city life. Thus, Lucy is less lonely than she had anticipated, and had felt more settled than ever even before meeting Carol.

"Did I say 'losers'? I meant…" Jase is still not quite at his ease with her. After all, Lucy is a sophisticated older woman with an exotic personal life. "I meant… 'under-achievers'."

"Well, I suppose that's slightly more accurate."

"I like what you've done with the place." Jase is impressed with her living-room. Not so much the girly wall-hangings, and vague odour of lavender. The wide-screen TV, state-of-the-art hi-fi, and multi-media computer are more his thing. "Lab assistants must get paid more than I thought."

"It's amazing what you can afford when you don't have to worry about… well… family stuff." And don't spend all your money on drugs - Carol has filled her in re Jase's past. She puts on one of the tapes that Jase has brought round. It's the first of their Sunday ones. The crystalline clarity of the reproduction is merciless in laying bare their deficiencies, but Lucy smiles. "Wow. It certainly exceeds my expectations. Although they were pretty low, to be honest."

"See what I'm saying? This could actually work!"

"I never doubted it." This makes Jase blush. "I just didn't think it'd start coming together so quickly."

"Yeah, well, that's what happens when you steal other people's songs." Jase sighs. "Instead of spending years putting your heart and soul into trying to write your own, which turn out to be crap, anyway."

"Ah. 'I've suffered for my art – now it's your turn!'"

"That's the kind of thing." Jase makes a face at his solo on "Grapevine". "Oops. Exactly the same as the one in 'Ain't No Sunshine'. I'll have to watch that."

Similar terse musicological analyses follow as they sit listening to their handiwork. Otherwise, between them there is an uneasy silence.

"You, er…" Lucy is regretting the remark even before she has properly formulated it. "You don't seem to be very good at conversations that aren't about music."

A shy grin. "Oh, well, I'm pretty much a moron when it comes to anything else."

"But… weren't you going to go to university?"

"Yeah. Film Studies, I was going to do. Wouldn't want to study music." He shudders. "What if it started to piss me off? My whole life would stop making sense. The entire internal structure of my mind would start to crumble. I'd become a husk. A zombie! An automaton! " He pauses. "Er, see what I mean about the moron thing?"

Alun is mildly intrigued when he opens the package on Thursday morning. The postcard is an advert for a lesbian-friendly health-screening service in Bristol. The message on the other side reads "Hi, Al. Copied the stuff from the weekend (the non-crap stuff) to CD – we thought you might fancy a listen. Jase said something about your mojo, which went way above my head. Till Sat. a.m. Love, Lucy." The title scrawled in blue pen on the disc reads "Ofnadwy Bluesville – the Wilderness Years".

"What's that?" This is his companion from the previous night, an East European woman he picked up in a bar in Cardiff. "Bootleg compact discs? Is this how you make your money?"

"I don't have any money, love." As he'd spent most of the evening trying to persuade her, but she decided to come home with him anyway.

He waits until he has driven her to the station, parting only with a tenner for train fare and sundries, before slipping the disc into his car stereo. In the middle of the third tune, he pulls into a supermarket car-park, and sits there listening. When the disc reaches its end, he is unembarrassed to note that his eyes are moist.

"You've done what??!!" Violet starts at the ferocity of Jase's response to the voice on the other end of the line. But that voice belongs to his rat of a father, so she shouldn't really be surprised. It is Thursday afternoon, and Alun is calling from his office at the club. "Have you completely lost your fucking mind??!!"

"Jason! Language!"

"Sorry, Mum, but he's... he's only gone and..."

What Alun has done is to book Ofnadwy Bluesville to play in the function suite of the Affiliated on Sunday night. The Sunday night which is 70-odd hours away.

"But... I've got to work Sunday night!"

Alun has already taken care of this by phoning up his old mate Mo Khan, and asked if Jase can have the evening off, just this once. He has also had several A4 leaflets photocopied and distributed around all the local shops, as well as placing a small ad in the 'Entertainments' section of the local newspaper, for publication on Saturday.

"But... but Dad..."

"I know what you're gonna say, son. It's your band, you should be in control of these things. But..." He allows a note of pathos to creep into his voice. "Look, Jase... you know what I've been like this past year. I need to get back on the horse, mun. Back into the lion's den. If I don't get over this thing soon, I never will."

"But... it's *too* soon, Dad."

A world-weary sigh at the other end of the line. "Son – did I ever tell you the story of me and Marto, booked in to play this American Army base in East Anglia? Back in the early days, it was, we were still doing our 'eighties pop stuff. So we get there, amazing place it was, it was. And this security guard bloke, he looks at us funny when we say who we are. For some reason, they were expecting a couple of black guys! 'Cause he's African-American, this bloke who's leaving, whose party it is. But we say, okay, no worries, must have been some breakdown in communications, but we've come this far, we'll give it a go, like. And we get in the hall, and start setting up. And the odd soldier pops his head round the door, every now and again, and looks at us funny. And they're all carrying guns. And Marto says to me 'I don't reckon we're going to get away with Spandau Ballet covers tonight, mate.' So, ninety minutes notice, we change the set. Completely. All Motown covers. "What Becomes of the Broken-Hearted", "I Second That Emotion", "Grapevine", "Just My Imagination Running Away With Me", "If I Were A Carpenter", loads of Stevie Wonder – Marto loved Stevie. Okay, so some of the lyrics were a bit ad lib. But we fucking stormed the joint! They loved us!" Jase can detect a smirk. "We both scored that night, as well."

"And your point is…?"

"My point is – you're a professional now, son."

"Nothing to do on Sunday night?

(Of course not – you live in Wales!)

Check out

OFNADWY BLUESVILLE

Unaffiliated Club, Funktion Suite.

Free Entry!!

Be there or be [] "

The poster is intended to betray Alun's punk roots, the name of the band being rendered as though from letters cut out of a newspaper, cf. a kidnapper's ransom note. It is embarrassment more than nerves which impels Lucy's hands to tremble as she creeps around the school, long before opening hours, pinning copies up on every noticeboard she can find. As she is admiring her handiwork outside the principal's office, a warm hand alights on her left shoulder.

"Oh, hello, Mr Protheroe."

"Lucy." Deputy Head Rhodri Protheroe would like to think that he is known around the school corridors as "Rhod of Iron". In actuality, his nickname is "Creeping Jesus". He peruses the poster. "An extra-curricular pursuit of yours?"

"Oh, well, I'm just the bass-player."

"Is this…" Protheroe weighs his words with insufficient care. "Is this some kind of… gay thing?"

"Not really, Mr Protheroe. Not unless the chemistry lab, for example, suddenly becomes gay as soon as I walk into it." She decides not to give him time to think about this. "You know Alun Hopkins."

"Oh, yes. I know Alun." Having ignored him at school, since he generally steered clear of the thickos. "Singing again, is he?"

"Well, it's his son's band. But, yes."

"Ah. Excellent. I'll be sure to…" And he slowly walks away, attempting to convey an impression of pensiveness.

Dai has been busy attending to his other interest, so when they convene for what was to have been their leisurely Saturday morning rehearsal, the news of their first gig comes as a complete surprise. "Tomorrow night?" He frowns slightly as the information takes hold. "Shit." The flicker of an eyebrow, and an almost imperceptible nod. "Okay. Cool." Ba-dum-tsh.

Jase hands out copies of the running-order he has spent the last two days honing. "First rule, son – don't have too many slow songs in a row."

"You haven't even read the fucking thing, yet!" This is the first complete sentence Jase has said to Alun today, having returned to customary son-to-father grunting mode. Alun raises a placatory hand, and they all study the list.

"Looks good to me." Lucy is the first to speak, not raising her eyes for fear of the crossfire.

Jase chooses to interpret the others' silence as an acquiescent one. "Right. We'll run right through, and only stop if there's a problem. Alright?"

They do so, the only difficulties being several Dai-oriented false starts to "Touch The Hem Of His Garment", and confusion over the key-change in "Don't Dream It's Over". "Don't Let Me Be Misunderstood" is muted, but a tacit agreement has arisen to the effect that they will only go balls-out on it in front of an audience.

"Can I ask you something, son?"

"Ask away." Jase is now somewhat cheerier than he was an hour ago.

"Do you want me to say anything between the songs?" Alun's patter during his Tom Jones act is legendary, for a variety of reasons.

"A smile, a joke, and a funny walk? I don't think so, Dad."

"I mean… I can't just say nothing! It's my club. People know me. If I tried to come across all moody, it'd be fake, wouldn't it?"

Jase considers this. "Just keep it simple, okay? The names of the songs, who we are, stuff like that. Oh - and do it in your own voice. Right?"

Alun assumes the hurt expression of an unfairly accused eight-year-old. "Dunno what you're talking about." He has been known to lapse into a Vegas drawl whilst in the footlights' glare.

They run through the songs once more, this time in a rather mechanical, lacklustre manner, the priority being to attain some fluency. Flair will come later, Jase reasons to himself, as they pack up. But is that a good thing? He's always been rather a fan of raggedness when it comes to live music. Always hating it when fellow gig-goers remark on the way out that, well, it was alright, but it didn't sound like the record. "So fucking stay at fucking home and listen to the fucking record, then!!", he never shouts in their smug, over-fed, moronic faces.

"We'll set up in the Unaffiliated, first thing, eh? If that's alright with you." This is Alun, taking charge, but pretending to defer to Jase.

"Okay. Open up around ten, alright?" This is Jase, taking charge, and deferring to no-one. "We'll run through once, so we can stay fresh. And everybody - have an early lunch, so we don't go on stage all bloated and yawny."

As it transpires, there is little chance of Jase feeling bloated on stage the following night, since, shortly after his Sunday lunch of burnt roast beef and packet mashed potato, he has an epic attack of diarrhoea. "Nerves", says his mother, who is an expert on the subject. Jase pulls himself together and goes for a walk, berating himself for being scared.

"It's only the upstairs room of some manky working-men's club in the middle of nowhere," he mutters. "No-one's going to turn up, anyway."

Although by the time he's got half-way to his favourite hill, three separate groups of people have greeted him, commenting on tonight's gig, and he's had to turn back, rush home, and go to the toilet again.

Sunday night, 21.05. Alun would have suggested going on late in any case, in order to ride the wave of frustrated anticipation, but Jase is in the toilet at the appointed time, the top of the hour. The rest of Ofnadwy Bluesville ascertain that he has made careful use of the ablutionary facilities before they do the handshake thing, which they've decided should become a *bona fide* ritual. The P.A. has been playing a soul- and punk-oriented tape put together by Jase – one consisting of blues standards might unduly raise expectations. But it is now quiet, and the natives are growing, if not exactly restive, increasingly curious, as the guys and gal make their way through the crowd and onto the tiny stage. Without a word, without even acknowledging the existence of the thirty or so assembled friends, relatives and vague acquaintances, they plunge straight into:

Song 1: "Yer Blues".

Met with enthusiastic applause, and the quizzical expressions of several younger attendees who have been told by their elders that it is a Beatles tune.

"Thank-you very much. We are Ofnadwy Bluesville, and this next song is called:

" 'Old Man Trouble'!"

Lucy's bass guitar heroics prompt several surprised, approving glances towards Carol, who is working behind the bar - Violet is taking care of baby Taylor, since she can't stomach the thought of the father and son reunion. Applause and cheers, as it finishes, but the audience decreases slightly, as a few of the elders, who'd secretly been hoping for a Woodward, slip downstairs for a quieter drink.

"Thank-you, thank-you, thank-you, ladies and gentlemen. Otis Redding, God rest his soul. God rest a lot of people's souls, looking down the set-list. You'll definitely know this one."

Song 3: "Ain't No Sunshine."

Met by rapturous applause, especially Jase's concluding guitar solo, which lasts only slightly longer than a minute.

"Jason Hopkins, ladies and gentlemen, fruit of my loins! And on the drums, Dai Williams! On the bass, Lucy…" he pauses, and glances over at her. She smiles, and mouths something at him. "Lucy Dyke? You cannot be serious." She rushes over and whispers in his ear. "Lucy Tyson! Just testing! And my name is Alun Hopkins!" A bad impression of a man being taken aback, as the few remaining members of his fan-club shout "Yay!". "Thank-you very much. We're going to speed things up, just a little now. 2, 3, and…"

Song 4: "Spooky".

During which, there is even a little dancing in the crowd, which is now approaching fifty, thanks to an influx of kids from Lucy's school. Alun signals for the guys to go straight into the next intro, while he drinks from his bottle of water.

Song 5: "Heartbreak Hotel".

Some puzzlement amongst the audience, who take some time to recognise the tune, and the reception is relatively subdued.

"Thank-you very much, ladies and gentlemen! Listen to me now – are you ready to testify?" More puzzlement. "I said – are you ready to testify?!" A few game calls of "Yes!" from the youthful element. "This one goes out to all you Jehovah's Witnesses out there!"

Song 6: "Touch The Hem of His Garment."

During which the dancing resumes, with greater conviction than before, the small area of moving bodies steadily expanding as the piece progresses. Much applause. Alun goes to Jase, puts a hand on his shoulder, whispers in his ear. Jase nods, and makes a twirling motion with his fingers to both Dai and Lucy, which mystifies them both until Alun announces: "Thank-you very much, ladies and gentlemen – there's going to be a slight change of running-order, which means nothing to you good people, of course, but I just thought we'd tell the rest of the band. This next tune is a classic, and it's from Wales!" A patriotic cheer.

Song 7: "No Matter What."

And the dancing continues, vindicating Alun's impulse to keep the tempo up. The audience now exceeds sixty, thanks to the late arrival of a curious Bumpy and Teg, whom no-one is about to eject, despite the fact that the Unaffiliated is now officially contravening fire regulations. "Cymru Am Byth" shouts Alun, inappropriately, waving a clenched fist in the air. There is little response. "Okay, we're going to take things down again, now. This one was written before even I was born, ladies and gentlemen."

Song 8: "Blues In The Night".

Jase notices some of the teenagers in the crowd listening with scholarly attention to Harold Arlen's 1942 lyrics, about how generally rubbish women are, delivered without a trace of ironic intent by his father. He thinks of his mother, sitting alone in front of Sunday night television, and is half a bar late coming in on his guitar solo, which seems to hit high notes he never knew he could reach. As it finishes, he is too busy wiping his eyes to acknowledge the roar of approbation. "Jase Hopkins, ladies and gentlemen!"

Song 9: "Don't Dream It's Over."

Now there are couples slow-dancing together, which doesn't happen often these days, even during the wedding receptions which the Function Suite is more accustomed to hosting.

"Ah, yes, ladies and gentlemen. That tune reminds me of the 1980s. Yessiree. I spent most of the early part of that decade working down a coalmine." A shout of recognition from men of a certain age. "Yeah, but unlike you, I hated every frigging second of it. Anyway, I want to dedicate this next song to the memory of my good friend Marto Cavanaugh…" A shout of recognition from men of a certain sexual persuasion. "Marto, who helped me on the road to showbiz mega-stardom." Awkward silence. "It's alright, love, I *am* joking."

Song 10: "I Heard It Through The Grapevine."

Alun is too genuinely choked up to speak at the end of this, and signals for the guys to move on.

Song 11: "Life's A Gas."

Moist eyes amongst the watching dozens, and another rapturous reception. Alun turns to the rest of Ofnadwy Bluesville, and pumps his fist, instructing them to cut the schmaltz, and raise the beef quotient.

Song 12: "Ain't No Love In The Heart Of The City".

Suitably robust, this energises everyone, which is a pity, since we are nearing the end. "Okay. Erm… a lot of these songs, I've never sung before, except in the bath, like." He winks at a woman in the front row. "You know, love, you were there." Laughter, tempered with discomfort at the possibility being that he might actually not be joking this time. "But here's one I've been singing for years. Not quite like this, though."

Song 13: "I'm Never Gonna Fall In Love Again."

Health and Safety go out of the window, as some of Alun's older devotees, who have been bemoaning the state of things in the downstairs bar, get a whiff of a Woodward, and storm the Suite. Excitement, succeeded by bemusement, resignation, and then a grudging respect.

"Thank-you, thank-you, thank-you. We are Ofnadwy Bluesville, you have been a marvellous audience, and after this one, we're all going for a curry!"

Song 14: "Please Don't Let Me Be Misunderstood."

The funky drummer, the posing crooner, the sparring bass and guitar soloists – it actually seems to work again, and Terpsichorean convulsions of all descriptions are occurring on the floor – from moshing amongst the kids, to hand-bag circling at the periphery, and even a handful of brave souls attempting what they imagine to be the Watusi. And maybe the band stretches things to within a minute or two of breaking point, for as they come together on the crashing final chord, there is whooping, and there is hollering, but there are no cries of "More!". They make their way through the throng greeted by warm pats on the back, rather than the frenzied ripping off of clothes.

Two minutes after they leave the stage, as Ofnadwy Bluesville are convened in the turns' dressing-room, sweating like hogs, Lucy strips down to her bra, paying no heed to the hungry male eyes of her fellow musicians. "That was fucking brilliant!"

Jase agrees, in a mumble, still striving to cope with sensory overload, emotional exhaustion, and the realisation that he may, finally, have managed to get something right. Alun, though bursting with pride on the inside, remains the measured veteran. "I've had better receptions. Not many, but... er – where's Dai?"

But they already know. Dai has gone off with Bumpy and Teg. Certain considerations being even more pressing than the contemplation of a classic, if flawed, first gig, over a mountainous Khan's Curry Kitchen House Special

YER BLUES

Biryani .

CHAPTER FIVE

Sonia is not a great fan of her body. Which, paradoxically, is why she spends a lot of time looking at it in the full-length mirror in her bathroom. The breasts are too small, the bottom too big, the legs too short. And she's starting to find grey hairs in the most improbable places. "That's not right, surely! I'm twenty-two years old!" She looks older, though. Those creases under her eyes. Inherited from her mother. Who already had two kids at her age.

She looks again at the clothes laid out on her bed. "Why does everything in my wardrobe look like a sack?" She sighs. "Because my body looks like a sack." She puts back the gipsy skirt, and retrieves her favourite pair of jeans. At least she knows she looks alright in jeans, as long as they aren't too tight. Although Michael always liked to clamp his hand on her arse, when they were walking out together. In the early days. When he still wanted to be seen with her.

She has plenty of perfume left over from Christmas. She normally prefers the smell of soap, but since she'll be in a smoky environment, a little help from the good people at Lentheric won't do any harm. And Givenchy, to be on the safe side. Not that it'll make much difference, anyway. Probably.

She has seen the band play twice before. The first time was just after Christmas, at an all-day concert in a pub up in the Valleys somewhere, a benefit for victims of the disaster in Asia. Michael was going with some of his drinking buddies, who were visiting from London. This being the period of their relationship during which he'd only go out with her to places where it would be impossible for them to talk – gigs, the cinema, out with friends. She doesn't remember much about most of the groups that played – she's more into soul than guitars. Given the crowd-pleasing nature of the event, though, there were plenty of amusingly inept versions of the hits of yesteryear, which was, at the very least, amusing.

The MC announces Ofnadwy Bluesville as "a band who's only been together a couple of months, but they're fast building up a reputation as a live outfit. I think some of you'll recognise the lead singer!" Sonia, through the beery haze, does not recognise the lead singer. He looks like a shorter, thinner, weasellier version of Tom Jones, and he sure knows how to work a crowd. In fact, they're a disparate bunch, appearance-wise. They've made an effort with the colour-scheme – all of them wearing something crimson; the singer's suit, the bass-player's blouse, the drummer's trousers and baseball cap, the guitarist's long t-shirt. But, otherwise, they might be in four different combos. The vocalist is obviously an old club singer, like Sonia's uncle Joseph in Trinidad. The bassist looks as though she's playing on a lesbian cruise-ship, the guitar-player is pure grunge, and the lad on drums… well, he might be in that cantina band in "Star Wars" for all that he knows what was going on. They play mostly familiar songs in a bluesy style, which would have been nothing more than a neat gimmick, were it not clear that they are taking it seriously, especially the spotty youth on the six-string, who closes his eyes when he plays a solo, but doesn't make fish-faces like the heavy-metal people Michael likes. Michael talks to his friends all through the Ofnadwy Bluesville set. The next band on is a teenage female vocal trio in very short skirts, who sing to a backing-tape. With a gleeful "wa-hey!", Michael joins his mates in pushing down the front, and Sonia orders a double vodka, thus losing most of the rest of the day.

The next time she sees Ofnadwy Bluesville, she and Michael are no more. Things hadn't been right since graduation, anyway. They had to move out of the student house they were sharing with two other couples, and he'd suggested that they get separate places, at least until things looked clearer. He was sensitive about financial matters, because Sonia had already secured employment with a small, local advertising agency, and he could only find bar-work. Not that he was looking for anything serious, since he was saving to go travelling. So, she found a cheap, rented flat, and he moved into another shared house, with four girls. Which should have raised her suspicions, but she's a trusting soul. Or was. Not because anything happened with the four girls, as far as she knew, but because a few weeks into the New Year, he told her it was over, moved back to Essex, became engaged to his secondary-school girlfriend, and got a job with her dad's printing firm, all thoughts of back-packing dismissed as a foolish young man's fancy.

The ad-agency's receptionist, Zara, had joined the firm at the same time as her, so, naturally, they palled up. But she has a steady boyfriend, and whenever she suggests an evening out, it is a given that they will be going as a trio, which makes Sonia feel irrelevant. But on one of these nights, they end up in the city-centre night-spot where Zara and Jake had first met, doing the Saturday night salsa thing. But this is a Wednesday, and there's a local band on, whose name does not register with Sonia until they begin playing that Beatles song. This time, Ofnadwy Bluesville are all wearing identical crimson shirts, in quality cotton. Although the drummer's is draped over his shoulders, the bassist's unbuttoned such that one can plainly see her sports bra, and the singer's gradually growing darker and darker as he perspires liberally under his black suit. The guitarist's shirt is untucked, and flowing free, almost kaftanesque over his skinny frame.

It wasn't that Sonia hadn't got it the first time. It was the blues. Her brother Carl, four years older, had gone through a blues phase in his teens, and filled the upstairs of the house with blistering guitar noise before discovering that girls preferred disco. Some of these songs are mere pop tunes. But what the band are doing is breathing fresh life into them by reacquainting them with their blues roots. Especially the guitar-player. And while he is pallid, with bad skin and a mournful set to his mouth, when he is in mid-solo, and plainly finding his bliss, he might almost be mistaken for a good-looking person.

Zara and Jake have to go home early, so that they can indulge in energetic sex and still get a full night's sleep before work in the morning. Sonia surprises them by deciding to stay, declining their offer of a lift home. After all, her flat is only a half-hour's walk away, and the streets are well lit, and not as lousy with adolescent drunks as they might have been on a Friday or Saturday.

The first time Sonia had seen the band, they only played for half an hour, mostly focussing on songs from the 1970s. Tonight, though, it's the full show, culminating in a version of "Don't Let Me Be Misunderstood" which, while eccentric, manages to wring shrieks of approval from the jaded mid-week crowd. "Thank-you very much, we've been Ofnadwy Bluesville, you've been beautiful, g'night!"

It is a late bar, so she hangs around, consuming vodka-based fruit-flavoured drinks as if there were no tomorrow. At length, the singer of the band appears, and makes for the bar. He is intercepted by two women, who rush from opposite sides of the room to engage him in conversation. Sonia notices the way he casually rests his hand on the younger blonde's pelvis, inclining his head so that he can both hear what she is saying, and gaze directly into the freckly cleavage of the older blonde. Obviously a master of his art. Sonia pictures the scene as a poster, advertising some health tonic for the over-fifties - caption: "He's still got it!"

At her next trip to the bar, she is surprised to find herself standing next to the band's girl bass-player. Sonia taps her on the arm. "You were good."

The bass-player smiles. "We aim to please." She seems prettier and less butch than on stage.

Sonia fumbles for something to say. "I've seen you before, I think. A charity thing?"

"Yeah?" the bass-player shrugs. "Charity's good. But I quite like getting paid, as well." Her drinks arrive – one beer, one water. "Cheers."

Sonia does not turn to watch the musician go, but wonders if she is being checked out. Not that she's ever been tempted by the concept of lady-love, but at this stage in her emotional life, she might as well keep her options open. At this point, a middle-aged Rasta tries to chat her up, asking her if she's African. She puts on her broadest Wolverhampton accent, which somehow succeeds in putting him off.

On the way back to her seat, she sees Ofnadwy Bluesville's guitarist and bass-player sitting, huddled together at a corner table. Their heads are almost touching as they converse intently. Sonia feels a pang of something indefinable on noticing that the girl's hand is on the boy's knee.

She does not stay for much longer.

It is a few weeks later that events conspire to turn her into an Ofnadwy Bluesville groupie.

Having now tuned into the name, she starts seeing it in local listings. They get a mention virtually every week in the gig guide on the Radio Wales blues show, even when they're playing in Edinburgh or Norwich. She buys a three-CD box set featuring people with names like Furry Lewis and Howlin' Wolf, and is captivated.

One Saturday morning, she drives her Skoda several miles up the A470, on work business – taking photographs of the post-industrial landscape, in order to maintain the currency of the agency's database of picturesque local images. Having had limited success, due to the fog, she pops into a supermarket to pick up a can of diet cola. As she is wandering through tinned foods, she passes a young couple with a baby. She has to look twice before she realises that the companion of the badly-dyed red-head with the voice like fingernails down a blackboard is the girl bass-player, all in black denim, making funny faces at the child, which is in the carrier secured to her chest. The bass-player does not notice her, and why should she? Interesting, thinks Sonia.

Even more interestingly, back in Cardiff that afternoon, she notices a tall, lank-haired, cadaverous figure, hunched over the miserly blues section in Virgin. She circles the aisle twice before contriving to rifle through the section next to his - Songs From The Shows. "Excuse me – aren't you in that band?"

Jase looks at her, startled. "Erm… yes," he replies. A micro-second later, realising that she might have mistaken him for someone in another band. "Ofnadwy Bluesville, you mean?"

"That's right." Well, obviously.

"Seen us play, have you?"

"Yeah. Twice. You're a good guitar-player." No matter how often she replays this in her head, later, it always sounds as though she's somehow surprised.

"Yeah, well." He grins, lop-sidedly. "I practise a lot, by myself, like."

"Don't we all?" She says this without thinking, and starts to giggle like an unstable child. "Sorry, that was gross."

Covering her discomfiture, Jase points to the CD she's randomly picked up. The soundtrack to "Carousel". "Hey – have you heard the Roland Kirk version of that song… what's it called…", he slides his finger down the case, "… 'If I Loved You'?"

"Erm… Roland…?"

"Roland Kirk. Blind black jazz sax-player. Used to play two at a time, sometimes. Just showing off, like. Really good version, it is. The one I've got, it's live, and at the end, with the audience cheering, someone shouts out 'That was mean! That was mean!' Classic."

Sonia has calmed down a little. "So, you're really a jazz fan, are you?" She's on slightly safer ground, here, having had a brief George Duke/Roy Ayers phase during her A-levels.

"Not really. I just know good art when I hear it, like." He winces, conscious that he is saying "like", too often. "Hey – we're playing the Barfly in a couple of weeks. You should come down. Bring some friends."

"Yeah. Yeah, I'll do that." She extends a hand. "Sonia."

He reciprocates. "Jason."

And before she realises it, they have disengaged, he has moved on to the budget DVDs, she has replaced "Carousel" in the wrong rack, and that is that.

Tonight is the night. She's meeting Zara, Jake, and maybe a couple of others in a wine bar before the gig. Having decided on the jeans, Sonia must now find the right top. The obvious thing would be one with a band name on, but she grew out of all of the ones she had, both literally and figuratively, several years ago. A rugby shirt? Inappropriate, since she knows nothing about the game. But there's the Wolverhampton Wanderers football shirt that Michael bought her for her last birthday. Yes, that'll do. Nice and symbolic – out with the old, et cetera. Plus, the way the polyester clings makes her tits look passable.

Assembled in the bar are Zara and Jake, Greg, her senior colleague in the design department, his boyfriend Wahid, who works for the BBC, and, to everyone's surprise, Tim, one of the directors of the agency. It transpires that he knows Alun, Ofnadwy Bluesville's lead singer, of old. Not only were they at school together, but when he was working for his old firm, Alun performed his Tom Jones act at one of their Christmas parties, and somehow managed to get off with the M.D.'s barely legal daughter in between drinking and reminiscing with Tim. "That was before the coronary, of course. Not too long before, come to think of it."

Sonia is mildly horrified when, after serious prompting and pointing to her watch, the youthful contingent decides that it's having more fun drinking cocktails and bitching about minor celebrities than it would in some squalid cellar. And anyway, blues music's for old people. "That's my cue", says Tim, grabbing his ridiculously expensive leather jacket.

She feels slightly awkward walking with him, mainly because a single misplaced comment might cost her her job, but also because she's not sure of his motives. It seems unlikely that he fancies her, but you never know. "So – why didn't your wife come out tonight?"

"What? Margaret in the same room as Alun Hopkins?" He chuckles. "I don't think so. Not after the last time." The Christmas party. Where Alun groped her, before catching sight of fresher meat. "Funny, she didn't tell me till a couple of days later. Between you and me, I think she was slightly upset that he... you know... moved on." This was a period during which Tim and Margaret were trying out the open marriage thing.

"Er – how did that work out for you?"

"I had a ball. Hence the coronary."

They arrive at the Barfly just in time for Sonia to avoid becoming privy to too much information. The support act is a bunch of art students from Newport, doing a Rolling Stones tribute act as part of a video project. Even though Sonia has been out of university for less than a year, she is astounded at how young and optimistic they all look. She goes to the bar to get Tim a fruit juice and herself a lager. As she turns to go back to where her boss is standing, trying not to look uncomfortable, she bumps into the bass-player from Ofnadwy Bluesville. "Oops – sorry. Oh, hello, again."

Lucy just about remembers her. "Oh, yeah. The salsa place."

Lucy explains that amongst the Stones people is a former pupil at the school where she works, in the Valleys. They've done a deal whereby in return for letting them open the show, they'll be videoing their set to enable Ofnadwy Bluesville to put a couple of performances on their website – "actually, it's my website" - in order for promoters to see what they can do. The students will also constitute the bulk of the screaming audience.

"Erm, isn't that slightly dishonest?"

"Your point being…?"

When Sonia brings Tim his drink, there is an interested expression on his face. "Who was that?"

Sonia explains.

"I see. She, er, looks a bit gay. Are you… close?"

"I'm not a lesbian, Tim."

Tim does not speak again until the teenage Jagger has performed his final curtsy. "Amazing to think that as old as I feel, the real Bill Wyman could actually be my father. Age-wise, I mean."

One might expect most of the students who don't need to stay for decency's sake to begin filtering out, but a good few remain. The venue also starts filling up with a surprising number of older music-lovers, Ofnadwy Bluesville's more accustomed constituency, so that by the time the band goes on, the joint is just about ready to jump.

And jump it does.

As "Please Don't Let Me Be Misunderstood" reaches its usual feverish conclusion, the approbation is deafening. Even Tim looks ten years younger, despite the damage being done to his jacket by exposure to the sweat, smoke and inferior fibres of his co-celebrants. "That was fucking awesome!"

"I told you they were good."

"Yes, Sonia. But you didn't tell me they were fucking awesome!"

As the bulk of the audience makes for the exit, Tim gestures in the direction of the bar, and wonders if Sonia wouldn't mind sticking around a bit, so he can have a chat with Alun. Sonia doesn't tell him that she never had any intention of leaving. He buys her another lager, and risks a vodka-tonic, as they watch the drummer, mysteriously transformed from rock'n'roll animal to dazed blank canvas, dismantling his kit. "So – I wouldn't have thought this was your kind of thing?"

"No?"

"I mean, all the black kids I know – that is to say, all the black kids my kids know – they're all into rap and r&b, and nothing else."

"Well… I'm not a kid."

"Sonia – when you're my age, everybody under thirty is a kid."

Presently, Alun emerges, eyes peeled for totty. He spots Tim. "Bloody hell, mate – what brings you to a dive like this?"

"Just wanted to see what you've been reduced to. What happened to the Tom Jones bit?"

"It's the boy. He was worried about my street credibility." Alun glances at Sonia's bosom, and is unimpressed. "Alright, love?"

The two men start to discuss the shortcomings of their grown-up children. Jason and Lucy return, and start to pack away their gear. Sonia watches them for a while before wandering over.

"Hey – you were really good."

Jase reddens. "Oh. Right. Thanks. I think we wobbled a bit in the middle, but nobody seemed to notice."

"Perfectionist? Pain in the arse? You decide." Lucy chuckles.

"Erm… can I buy you a drink? Erm… both of you?" As the pair look at one another. "Erm… all of you." As the drummer glances over.

Sonia is despatched for two beers, and a water for Jase, who is tonight's designated driver. Alun and Tim have been joined by two of the female art students, with Tim pontificating on the link between video art and advertising, and Alun trying to ascertain whether university bed-hopping is as rife as it was in his day. "Not that I actually went to university, like. Not to study, anyway."

Sonia and the rest of Ofnadwy Bluesville adjourn to a corner table, where Dai the drummer promptly falls asleep. Jase and Lucy treat her to a history of the band, which doesn't last long, and the conversation fizzles out.

"It… it must be weird, though. Having to tell your dad what to do."

"Oh yeah – he's finding it a real struggle", laughs Lucy as she checks her phone messages. "Oh, bugger. Carol." She goes and stands in the stairwell to make her call.

"Girlfriend?", suggests Sonia.

"Yep." Jase takes a casual sip of his water. "Why? Were you interested?"

"No, I… I mean… I'm sure she's very nice. But I prefer… you know… blokes."

"Oh. Right." Instinctively Jase glances over to where his father and Tim are still failing to impress the laughing student-birds. "Takes all sorts, I suppose."

"So, it must be… you must get lots of… being in a band… your girlfriend must get jealous."

Jase shrugs. Since the Ofnadwy Bluesville adventure began, he has had two sexual encounters. The first was with an old flame, who came up to him after an early pub gig. "Remember me?" They went back to hers, and did the deed on her parents' living-room floor. Lying there afterwards, he remembered that she had dumped him originally for someone whom she supposed must be more interesting, because he had a motor-bike. He thanked her, said goodbye, then went home and wrote a poem called "Emptiness", which he later threw away. The second was in a guest-house in North Wales, when Alun brought two middle-aged music-lovers back to the room they were sharing, and while he had sex with one, the other, to pass the time, offered to do Alun with her mouth. He agreed, since he was too drunk not to.

"I haven't got a girlfriend."

Dai raises his head, and squints at Sonia, eyes red. "Music is his lady, like. Lady-like. Like a lady? No, thanks, I am otherwise engaged." He collapses once more into the table.

"Rock and roll lifestyle, eh", ventures Sonia.

Jase gently ruffles his friend's hair. "He's a fuck-up. But he's my mate. So, what do you do, then? For work, like?"

"Design. For an advertising agency. But I'm a painter, really." This is the first time she's ever said this out loud, despite the fine art degree.

"You should paint my dad. In the nude."

"Ooh, I think I'd keep my vest on." This makes Jase laugh. "Anyway   - you've got a more interesting face."

"Ugly, you mean."

"You're not ugly." She lowers her eyes. "Anyway, I'm not one to talk."

"You reckon?" Jase tilts his head to one side. "You look like a bit like that Tamara Dobson. Out of 'Cleopatra Jones'."

"Why? Did she have a stupendously big arse as well?"

"Yours isn't that big." Jase has taken every opportunity to verify this – in the record-shop all those days ago, and at the bar tonight before she saw him, and when she was coming back from the toilet towards the end of "Heartbreak Hotel". "Not that it's any of my business, anyway."

They have faded into silence once more when Tim comes over. "Hey, Sonia..." He pauses, not having recognised the subdued, non-performing Jase at first. "Oh – excellent guitar-playing, man. Truly."

"Sure. Yeah. Cheers." Jase is still getting used to the idea of being complimented.

"Your dad's really proud of you, you know?"

"Yeah?" A half-smile. "That must be very nice for him."

"Listen, Sonia – I'm just about to phone for a taxi. Coming?"

Sonia looks over towards the bar. Alun and the two girls have disappeared. "Erm... it's okay, I can make my own way back."

"Are you sure?"

"Absolutely."

"Right, then. See you in the morning." He leaves, dodging past Lucy, who is still busy on the 'phone.

"He's my boss," explains Sonia.

"So, you don't live far, then?"

"Walking distance."

"That must be nice. Cardiff by night. Not much doing where we live. We have to make our own entertainment, like." He indicates the dozing Dai.

Lucy hangs up, and returns to the table. "We'd better get going. After all, some of us have got work in the morning."

"Yeah. Right." Jase gets up, and goes with her to the corner where their instruments are stacked. Or, rather, half-way to the corner. Sonia watches as Lucy stops, takes his arm, whispers in his ear, and jerks her head in Sonia's direction. Jase looks back, and sees her looking at him. Sonia raises her bottle in salutation. He ambles back to the table. "Listen, erm, maybe we could get together some time, you know, talk about music, and that."

"Yeah. That sounds good."

"Except… well, I work most evenings. Apart from when I'm doing band stuff."

Sonia produces one of the semi-serious business cards she's made up for herself at work. "This is my mobile number."

Jase takes it. "Cheers." He starts to walk away, then turns back. "I'd better have another one. I'm always losing things, me."

While he and Lucy are busying themselves with their hardware, Sonia drains her bottle, and gets up. Dai is still resting his head on the table. "Erm… Dai?"

He raises a reassuring finger. "I'm alright, love. They won't leave me. I'm the fucking heartbeat of this band. I'm the Ringo. The Keith Moon. The John 'Bonzo' Bonham. The… the…" He starts to snore.

Sonia waves to Lucy and Jase, and makes her way up the stairs into the cool night air. She takes a few paces before punching the air and growling "Yes!". Even though she's not quite sure that she's actually accomplished anything. Or that whatever she may have accomplished is actually worth accomplishing.

She has not even started wondering when Jase is going to call, when Jase calls. It is the following evening. Which indicates that this boy is obviously too uncool for school.

"Hi, there. Erm – you doing anything Sunday?"

"Erm… I haven't got any plans."

"Do you know anywhere we could go for Sunday lunch? It's ages since I had a decent Sunday lunch."

So, what to wear for a first Sunday lunch with someone you might, at some point in the near future, decide to sleep with? Jase decides on a pair of suit trousers, and a Morrissey sweatshirt, underneath his parka, it being cold and drizzly. Sonia goes for a long denim skirt, a flowery top, and a parka, which happens to be identical to Jase's. It is for this reason that he smiles as he sees her waiting in the concourse of Queen Street station, something which makes him both feel and appear more relaxed than he otherwise might. Sonia smiles back, relieved that they've managed to recognise one another. She points at his coat. "Great minds, eh?" Taking command, she kisses him on both cheeks.

"So – where are we eating?"

It's a functional pub, large without being cavernous, quiet without being dead. He orders the chicken, she plumps for plaice. They both drink lager. In between the Barfly and now, Ofnadwy Bluesville have played one gig, in Swansea. "It was good. Very good. In fact, I'm getting slightly worried, like."

"What – paranoid that you're too good?"

"No, it's just… when we first got together, we gelled so quickly. And the only bad gigs we have are when the sound gear's fucked, or when Dai forgets what order the songs are in. And we can usually rise above that."

"Maybe it's making up for the fact that… you know." Sonia attempts to choose her words carefully. "You're a professional outfit. Rather than… you know… having lofty artistic ambitions."

"Yeah." Jase sighs. "I mean, that's exactly what I was aiming for. And it's great, I'm really loving it. We all are. We're even operating at a profit. Which is not something I thought I'd ever be saying about any kind of project I might be involved in. But…"

"You do have lofty artistic ambitions."

"Ambition. But no talent. Well, not that kind." He has spent the past few days reading up on the visual arts. "I mean, there are thousands of decent Sunday painters. But only one Picasso. Only one Van Gogh."

"I feel the same way, really. I mean, I was never going to be a great painter. These days it's all about ideas, rather than skill. Which is fair enough. Portraits and chocolate box landscapes are all very well, but people need a kick in the arse every now and again. Except all I'm good at is portraits and chocolate box landscapes."

"I hear you, sister." Jase feels more at ease than he might have expected to. Perhaps it was the joint he smoked before leaving to catch the train. Or perhaps it's simply that he's with someone who makes him feel at his ease. Which is not something that happens very often. "Lucy's quite creative, though. She says she's going to write a concerto for bass guitar, one day. Even though she can't read music. It shouldn't be too difficult, on the computer."

"So, have you known Lucy long?"

"Not very."

"You seem… you're good mates, aren't you?"

"Yeah. I think I love her. A bit." Jase surprises them both with this. "I don't think I've loved many people in my life. Mam, of course. Dai. My dad, I suppose, even though he's… we've got a complicated history, me and my dad. But Lucy… it's just nice having a woman I can be close to without the sex thing getting in the way."

"Plus, being a lesbian, she can give you tips on…" She can feel her face growing hot. "What women like."

This is exactly what Jase and Lucy were discussing on the drive back from Swansea. With Alun interjecting his own brand of profane irrelevancy.

"So, er, what's it like working in advertising?"

"Well, it's not as glamorous as it sounds."

"It sounds about as glamorous as working in a bank."

Sonia chuckles, and talks about her job, her ambitions, such as they are, her life at university, and Michael. "Strange – you think you're in love with someone, then they leave, then you wonder if you really loved them at all. And if you didn't, what's the point of anything, anyway?"

"It's like my Mam and Alun. I'm sure if they'd stayed together, they'd have split up. If you see what I mean. But just because he ran off before she was ready for him to run off, she's let it cripple her. Emotionally, like."

"Well, no-one's ever going to do that to me." This emerges in a harsher tone than Sonia had intended. But Jase smiles.

"I know what you're saying." It is now Jase's turn to spill his guts. About the drugs, Dai, Alun's bad example, his mother's cooking. "Bloody hell – this must be the longest conversation I've ever had that wasn't about music, or films. With a girl, anyway. Is that sad, or what?"

"I feel honoured."

By now, it's time for dessert. "Now, I don't know much about women – but I know you aren't going to order a pudding, because you're worried about the size of your bum. But if I get one, you'll eat half of mine."

"I won't, if you order a cheesecake. Can't stand cheesecake."

Jase orders the cheesecake. Immediately it arrives, Sonia reaches over, digs her spoon in, and scoops up a good mouthful. "Oi!"

"I lied." She shrugs. "It's a tough old world."

Jase laughs, but gobbles up his dessert with ungentlemanly haste. "Another beer?"

As they sup their lager, the pub starts to fill up with a boisterous element. Forcing them to contemplate the fact that it is now almost evening. "So, er, are you working tonight?"

"No. Not tonight." For a couple of months, now, Jase has been part-time at the Khans, allowing them to give another feckless Valleys youth the chance to put "delivery-driver", "catering industry" and "race relations" on his CV. "Why? Have you got any plans?"

"Not really. Might do some reading."

They kill time talking about books, unsurprisingly finding several areas of convergence. When the atmosphere starts to grow too smoky, they decide to make a move, splitting the bill down the middle, even though the fish cost more than the fowl. "Let's just say you owe me a beer." Jase basks in his magnanimity.

Once outside, they start to walk in the general direction of the station. Sonia notices a poster advertising dance music nights at the Welsh Club. "Hey – have you ever thought about doing dj-ing? You could make good money. Especially if you don't just play the same old…"

"Listen… Sonia…" Jase comes to a halt, taking hold of her elbow. "Do you mind if I do something."

Before she can reply, he has bent down and is kissing her on the lips. It is over before she fully realises what is happening.

"Sorry. Just felt like getting it out of the way, like."

She gulps, still breathless. "Getting it out of the way?"

"I mean… the thing about… whether we're just going to be mates, meeting for a drink, and talking about… music and films. Or… you know. Anything else."

"Oh." Sonia is still composing herself. "Why? What do you want?"

"I think I've just told you." He starts to lose any composure he may have managed to fool himself into thinking he had. "But… the other thing… the friends thing… that'd be fine. I mean, you're good to talk to. If… you know. It's just going to be about talking."

Sonia decides to take control again. "Why don't we discuss this over a coffee? Back at mine?"

Twenty minutes later, they are standing on either side of her bed, looking at one another's naked bodies. "I know – nothing to write home about", they both think, apologising with their eyes, before slipping underneath the duvet.

Afterwards, they lie on their backs, hand in hand. "Sorry", he says.

"What for?"

"It wasn't very good. I haven't done it that often."

"I've had worse. Trust me." She gives his fingers a squeeze. "What were you thinking about?"

"I was thinking how beautiful you are."

"What were you really thinking?"

"I was trying to remember the full names of Glamorgan County Cricket Club's entire Championship-winning squad for 1997."

"Oh. Cricket gets you going, does it?"

"No, it doesn't. The exact opposite. That was kind of the point."

"Ah." She turns, and kisses his face. "You're cleverer than you look."

"Actually, I got that one from my dad. Just from general conversation, like. I didn't ask his advice, or anything."

"Glad to hear it." She rolls onto her side, and snakes an arm around his waist. They fall asleep, not thinking about cricket.

They awake just after eleven that night, get up, go to the bathroom, watch a little television, drink herbal tea, and return to bed, where Jase tries out some of Lucy's handy hints, which seem to work.

CHAPTER SIX

"This isn't going to affect the band, is it?" This is a scowling Alun, at Ofnadwy Bluesville's next rehearsal.

Even Dai is stunned. "You what?"

"The fact that he's got himself a bird. He'd better not let it mess up what we've got with the band."

Lucy chuckles. "What, you mean if he's not miserable any more, he won't be able to play the blues properly?"

Jase raises his hand. "Erm – I am actually in the room, you know?"

"I am not going to let us start turning down gigs because you'd rather be shagging." His vehemence startles them all, himself included.

"And what about all the gigs we've accepted for the exact same reason? Like Newcastle." Lucy scrunches her face into an Alun-esque leer. "'Yeah, let's do that one. I've never had a Geordie piece. They're supposed to be really filthy up there.'"

"It's not going to affect the band, Dad. I mean, I need the money, don't I?" He smiles, shyly. "What with having a bird, and everything. Okay, 'Your Cheating Heart', let's go."

Since the early days, Ofnadwy Bluesville have tweaked their repertoire. They've added a handful of tunes: Hank Williams' afore-mentioned country classic; "Anyone Who Had A Heart", which they finally managed to nail; and Joni Mitchell's "Carey", another of Lucy's suggestions. These are the up-tempo ones, at least the way they tackle them. There are also a couple of slowies: "Almost Blue"; "Wild Hearts Run Out Of Time", a late-period Roy Orbison, which Alun remembered from "Insignificance", a film about Marilyn Monroe meeting Albert Einstein which he'd gone to see when it came out in the 1980s in the forlorn hope of seeing some tit, coming out instead with a workable knowledge of the theory of relativity; and "You Don't Know What Love Is", from Billie Holiday's "Lady In Satin", Dai's favourite album of all time, but one which he can't listen to very often because her heroin-ravaged voice is a painful reminder of his own situation. They've also reluctantly abandoned "Spooky", because Alun can't help but sing it in a cheeky-chappie manner, which means it doesn't sit well with their other material. This leaves them free to vary their setlist to some degree, although the core numbers ("Yer Blues", "Trouble", "Garment", "Grapevine", "Ain't No Love", "Fall In Love", "Misunderstood") never escape a hammering, constituting as they do their cut-down show for support slots, festivals and the like.

It is a festival in Belgium, their first trip outside the UK, which threatens to prove the first point of conflict between Jase's bird and Jase's band. "Erm... I've got a couple of days off owing", Sonia points out, coyly. "And I've never been to Belgium."

Jase accedes without squaring it with the rest of the band, which leads to some prickly moments at their next meeting.

"I've seen it before, a thousand times." Alun is the primary objector. "Bit of quim comes along, you take your eye off the ball, you lose focus, things start falling apart."

"Dad – we are not The Beatles."

But even Lucy has her doubts. "Don't get me wrong, I really like Sonia. It's just... we don't want you playing to impress her, instead of the audience."

"I don't play for the audience, Luce. I play for myself."

"But... it's like..." Dai is also concerned. "We're a gang, bro."

"Oh. Oh, I'm terribly sorry." Jase draws himself up to his full height, which he can manage to make look impressive if he's sufficiently outraged. "Mr Panic In Needle Park, Old Man Pussy-Hunter, and Ms-Always-On-The-Phone-

To-Her-Fucking-Wife are scared that I, whose band this is, lest we forget, will cease to take my music seriously because of outside concerns? Well, pardon me for having a fucking life!" He storms out of the room, returning within ten seconds. "Erm… you do know she can drive?"

"Well, why didn't you say so in the first place?"

As well as agreeing to take a turn at the wheel of the Blues-Mobile (in actuality, the Khans' knackered old Transit van, sold to them at a nominal price, and fixed up by Dai), and being named as official tour photographer (on-stage only) Sonia also ponies up for a hotel-room, so that she and Jase can enjoy some privacy during their two-night stay. In retrospect, though, as far as most of the party is concerned, Sonia included, the highlight of the trip is the time spent in the company of Chattanooga Charlie.

On first receiving the roster, Jase thinks there must be some mistake. Naturally, Ofnadwy Bluesville are well down the bill on both days, but Chattanooga Charlie appears to be the penultimate act on the Saturday, supporting some Scandinavian college-boy 1970s-throwback blues-rock outfit, who happen to have sold a few hundred thousand albums on the European mainland in recent months. On arriving, though, after a surprisingly trouble-free trip – although Alun almost gets himself beaten up by the husband of a woman he tries to chat up in the bar on the ferry, and the customs officer gives the tottering Dai some suspicious looks as they pass through on the French side ("I had been hoping for a full-body search – I'll be contacting my M.P. when I get home") – they discover that there has been no error.

"It's scandalous", Jase insists.

The woman in the festival office agrees, on an artistic level. "But, hey, if we don't make money, it's no festival next year, so…" A Gallic shrug, although in those parts, no-one risks describing it as such.

Ofnadwy Bluesville have the task of livening up the joint after a late-afternoon lull occasioned by a Flemish comedy folk troupe, and their short set is ecstatically received, such that they are almost tempted to break their "no encores – leave them wanting more" rule. As usual, though, Dai has already gone AWOL, and the clamour subsides while Lucy and Alun are arguing over whether he and Jase should go on and do the acoustic version of "It's Not Unusual" that they've been playing with as a joke during rehearsals. The moment gone, Alun makes his way into the crowd to try out his "Do you have any Welsh in you? Would you like some?" line, and Jase, Sonia and Luce wander around the backstage area, looking for vaguely famous faces to casually hang around next to.

And then they see him, sitting in a deckchair next to a woman who looks like a seventy-year-old version of Gwyneth Paltrow. Skin like an autumn leaf, eyes blinking confusedly behind a pair of serious bottle-bottom spectacles, leaving through a copy of "Motor-Homes Monthly" magazine. Jase marches straight up to him. "Excuse me, sir, sorry to bother you, but I just wanted to say hello, and… and thank-you for the music."

The old man looks up, frowning. "Me? You sure?"

The story of Chattanooga Charlie is one of the more unusual blues fables. What has never been in doubt is that he was born in Tennessee shortly before the end of World War One. Not actually in Chattanooga, but in a Black settlement called Hortense; though dubbing himself Hortense Charlie was never an option. The family moved to Chattanooga in the early 1920s, and he grew up dirt-poor, and segregated from equally dirt-poor whites. His mother, who was a maid in the house of a prosperous Jewish businessman, brought home a guitar one day, which had been discarded by the family's son, who didn't have the patience to persist with it, despite having begged for one as a Christmas present. Charlie, the middle child of the five who survived, immediately took to it, and by his late teens was a fixture at local parties and dances. Early in 1940, he cut two 78s, "Catfish Creek"/ "Don't Know How" and "What's Mama's Little Baby Gonna Do Now"/ "Lonely Boy Blues", the latter pairing inspired by the death of his mother from pleurisy. Released on a small, Caucasian-owned label, they were minor hits throughout the South.

This is where the confusion begins. According to the story which became common currency, overcome by melancholia, Charlie left home and became a hobo, travelling from ghetto to ghetto, scraping a living singing and playing the guitar in the street. He was "discovered" several times, but, convinced that The Lord took his mother because he was making money from propagating the Devil's music, he never kept appointments for recording dates, always moving on without a word re his destination. He also restricted himself to devotional songs. He had to have a foot amputated after an accident which occurred when he failed to successfully negotiate a leap between two railroad cars. Nevertheless, he spent the next forty years hobbling around the Southern States, playing for his supper, sleeping in hay-barns and doorways, all the time developing a guitar style that remained pure because of his refusal to listen to pop music. It wasn't until the early 1980s that a white blues historian tracked him down, living in an old folks' home in Nashville, acquainted him with the several thousand dollars that he had accrued from the inclusion of his 1940 recordings on various Tennessee blues compilations – or at least, what was left of it after the usual music industry rip-off merchants had taken their various ten per cents – and persuaded him to record an album of new material and return to the road, this time playing respectably-sized venues on the blues circuit. His profile was enhanced when a sample of "Lonely Boy" featured on a multi-million-selling rap album, and the mainstream media started to take an interest.

It is at this point that the legend begins to unravel. An atypically assiduous New York rock journalist starts to dig and, flabbergasted at what he discovers, teams up with a friend in television, and confronts the bluesman as part of a breathless, hour-long documentary entitled "The Chattanooga Charlie Story".

Charles Whitworth did indeed leave home in the early 1940s. He joined the United States Army shortly before the Pearl Harbour incident, and became part of the only Black unit to fight in Europe, losing his foot while on active service in Italy, in the summer of 1944. Taking advantage of the G.I. Bill, and his compensation settlement, he went to study music formally at a local college, following which he became a high-school music teacher, spending the next forty years quietly ensconced in a small Tennessee town, living in relative suburban comfort, marrying twice, and watching the world change whilst introducing hundreds of students - in later years, many of them white - to the joys of classical guitar music. He tried to keep Chattanooga Charlie a secret, whilst pocketing his meagre royalties, but a former pupil who had become a record company executive in Los Angeles came upon his old recordings, and formulated a plan to re-introduce the now-retired Mr Whitworth to the music business, by selling a more heritage-industry-friendly version of the Chattanooga Charlie myth to cult music fans, and blackmailing a failing rapper into incorporating one of his old teacher's songs into a song about the medical and financial benefits of masturbation.

In the event, the TV documentary came to the conclusion that the scam had been a harmless one, signing off with the question: "Who is the real hero of African-American history? Chattanooga Charlie the blues cliché, or Charles 'Teach' Whitworth, the quiet revolutionary?" Blues purists, furious at having been duped, plumped for the former option, and embarked upon a campaign of vilification. This, in turn, energised the hip rock and hip-hop communities, who began to invite him to support them on their tours and play on their records, at least until the next roots sensation came along.

It has been a good decade and a half since Chattanooga Charlie's brief moment of cool came to an end. He has spent the intervening time doing what he should have been doing all those years earlier: travelling the world. But in an expensive RV, accompanied by a glamorous third wife, and regularly acclaimed by aficionados as a genius - in recent times, it has become increasingly evident that his guitar style owes as much to Segovia as to Skip James, and his stock has risen amongst serious lovers of music.

Jase, Sonia and Lucy spend a wonderful hour with the couple, sipping their first ever mint juleps, as mixed by Ingrid, a former cocktail waitress, and listening to Charlie's tales of music-biz high-jinks involving not Muddy Waters, or Blind Willie McTell, but Michael Stipe, Bruce Springsteen and L.L. Cool J.

They stick around to watch his set, which is greeted with unrestrained delight. As it transpires, this is his last European show – Chattanooga Charlie dies less than a month later, back home in the Deep South, taken by the cancer which, by rights, should have killed him ten years earlier.

The fact that Alun, when they all catch up with each other the following afternoon, is resolutely unimpressed by the Chattanooga Charlie episode, is but one source of tension within the group.

Another is the state Dai is in. Following the Saturday set, he falls in with a group of friendly Portuguese bikers, managing to sort out the knocking in the engine of one of their Harleys. As a reward, he is given strong drugs, and the use of one of their hefty women for a couple of hours. He returns to the modest, twin-bedded hotel-room he's sharing with Lucy at around three in the morning, and is still so deep in sleep at midday that she seriously fears that he has lapsed into a for-real coma. When he finally comes back to life, his speech is slurred, his eyes stare dimly into the middle distance, and his mouth is fixed in a permanent half-smile.

Jase and Sonia have a better time of things – an early night, plentiful good lovin', a healthy breakfast, a hand-in-hand stroll into town for some light shopping, an ice-cream brunch, and back to the hotel room for a quickie, before wandering down to the festival site, where they are greeted in the office by an apoplectic Alun. "Where the fuck have you been?"

Having been successful, the previous night, in enticing an easily-impressed Belgian girl back to his hotel-room, when he gets there he finds that he is all out of condoms – an absolute must, ever since he saw what Marto went through. He asks her to do him by mouth, but she only agrees to if he will do the same for her. He refuses, though, that not being part of his repertoire, at least not with hairy-legged strangers. She berates him in Flemish, throws the bedside lamp at him, breaking the bulb and hurting his shoulder, and stomps noisily out. He goes to the hotel bar, but there's no joy there - only ladies of the night, and he's never paid for it in his life; not directly, anyway. "Don't worry, Mr Hopkins", says the barman, "we have condom machines in the toilet." Alun drinks twelve ironic beers, and staggers up to his room, waking up only when the cleaners knock on the door in late morning and come in, startled to see a naked Welshman lying on a vomit-drenched blanket, dreamily caressing his erection.

When he returns to the festival site, Alun is informed that one of the acts has pulled out, and is asked if Ofnadwy Bluesville will go on a little later, and play a longer set, for a slightly adjusted fee. He immediately agrees, then feels guilty for taking on the responsibility without Jase's permission. He is then furious with himself for feeling guilty, then furious with Jase for not having his mobile phone turned on, then furious with himself for getting het-up and exacerbating his headache. And Lucy and Dai turn up, the lesbian with her forced cheerfulness, and the junkie looking like he's having an in-depth telepathic conversation with Gene Krupa. And then love's young dream floats in, only an hour before the band is due on.

"But it's not an hour. It's three hours, now."

"You weren't to know that, though, were you?"

"Dad – we have done this before. It's not a problem. Relax."

"Relax?!" The veins on the side of Alun's head start to bulge worryingly. "Re-fucking-lax??!!" He throws up his hands, and pushes roughly past Jase and Sonia, and out of the door of the Porta-Kabin. "I give up!"

He doesn't give up, of course, hooking up with the rest of Ofnadwy Bluesville half an hour before their set. He says barely a word to anyone, however, and it is not until he is taking his bow after the final flourish of "Don't

Let Me Be Misunderstood", that he turns to Jase and half-smiles, pointing to him so that the crowd can show their particular appreciation.

Under Sonia's stewardship, they manage to assemble for a meal in the hotel where she and Jase are staying; even Dai, who was in supreme drummer mode during the gig, but has now reverted to his post-Hell's Angels stupor.

"That's one of the best gigs I've ever seen you play." Sonia breaks one of many silences. "You should argue more often."

"Ooh, no." Lucy shudders. "I couldn't cope with the stress."

"It's called creative tension, dear", offers Alun. "I was always arguing with Marto. Well, arguing in his general direction. He never took much notice of me. Did his own thing, like." Completely out of the blue, he starts to cry. "It's times like this I really miss him, you know? Off on a foreign jolly. He fucking loved it. Totally... you know... lost his inhibitions."

"Maybe if he hadn't, he wouldn't have got the AIDS, like." This is Dai, momentarily returned to Planet Earth.

"I warned him! I tried to tell him!" Alun's fists are clenched impotently on the table. "'You don't know anything about my life', he said. Stupid bastard."

Twenty minutes later, after a half-bottle of Chablis, he is more his usual self. "See, what we've got with you two", as he spears the air, his dessert-spoon aimed at Jase and Sonia, "Is your basic ugly bloke and fat bird scenario. You see it all over the place."

Lucy gasps at his audacity. "Sonia isn't fat."

Jase rides the silence for a few seconds. "Yeah, thanks, Luce."

"No, I'm all for it. Good luck to you." Alun is unabashed. "Hey – this ice-cream's fucking gorgeous."

"Look, Dad – what is your problem?"

"Problem? I haven't got a problem. You aren't a lonely little wanker anymore. I'm pleased for you."

"No you're not."

"Look…" Alun sighs, deathly earnest. "I've just never been one for the cosy couple thing. It's just not me. That is my tragedy."

"I'm not like you, Dad. And believe me, that's no fucking tragedy."

Alun shrugs over-expansively to cover his hurt at this. "Like I say – I'm pleased for you. And Sonia… you seem like a very nice girl."

"Woman", interjects Lucy.

"Oh, shut up, you beaver-chomping freak."

"Hey – cool it, Al." This is Dai, continuing the return leg of his trip. "That's my sister's beaver you're talking about. Oh, shit, now I've got an image."

"Sonia – I like you. And I'm glad Jason's getting some tail at last. I just hope you're not fooling yourselves, that's all."

"Fooling ourselves? Fooling ourselves?!" Jase's face is contorted in uncomprehending fury. "We've been going out for two fucking months! I'm lucky if I get to see her twice a week! Fooling ourselves?! Chance'd be a fine fucking thing." He takes a large swig of wine. "You just want me to be unhappy because then you can pretend to yourself that I need you around. I come to you for words of wisdom once a year and you think, that's it. That's made up for twenty years of…" He shakes his head. "But you've heard it all before, right? Why don't you laugh in my face like you usually do?"

Alun chokes back the dismissive chuckle which was brewing. Silence reigns once more. Cue another attempt by Sonia to defuse the tension. "Is it because I is black?"

Lucy and Dai snort. Even Jase is starting to smile. But Alun leaps to his feet, sending his chair skidding across the room. "How dare you! How fucking dare you, you ignorant little cow!" And before anyone quite realises what is happening, he has walked out. No-one moves a muscle for several seconds.

"So, that's what he gets like when he hasn't been laid for a week." Lucy twiddles her imaginary mad scientist moustache. "Fascinating."

"It just pisses me off, though." The following morning, as Jase and Sonia lie huddled together in bed, he is still troubled. "Okay, yeah, he feels superior because he's spent his life shagging around, and I haven't. That's fine, I understand that. What I don't get is why women like someone who treats them like pieces of meat."

"Ah, but he doesn't." Sonia has seen Alun in action enough times to have got a handle on his technique. "He might think of them as pieces of meat. But when he talks to them, he makes them feel like sex-goddesses. If they let him." She kisses the warmth of Jase's neck. "When he doesn't fancy someone, he just ignores them. When he can't ignore them, he's all business-like. Like with the women at the club. He can't handle Lucy at all, for obvious reasons. And he can't cope with me because I'm in love with you." They have long since conquered L-word Peak. "He can't stand the competition."

"It's the haircut," says Jase.

"Oh, stop it." This irritates Sonia. First off, it was only an idle suggestion that Jase visit the hairdresser – he'd been whingeing about his appearance, as per usual, and how he might improve things. She'd joked that she didn't want him to improve things, and have to fight off hordes of other women. But if he was really serious, he could do something about his hair. And secondly, it wasn't, technically, a "hair cut". The hair was still long, as they both liked it. All the hairdresser had done – for a fee which shocked them both – was layer it, and deal with the greasiness, such that it now wafts when a wind catches it, rather than clinging obstinately to his shoulders. And thirdly – the knowing looks from Alun, Lucy, Dai, Carol, Violet. And even people who are just used to seeing him about the place. New woman? New hair? She's taken him in hand.

"He thinks I'm pussy-whipped. Which, to someone like him, is the ultimate indignity." Jase smiles to himself. "Still – I can think of worse things to be whipped by."

When the van arrives outside the hotel, Alun makes a point of getting out, trotting into the hotel lobby where Jase and Sonia are waiting, and picking up her suitcase. "Sonia – listen – sorry about last night. I was out of order."

"That's okay, Al. I didn't mean to offend you."

"I was just in a bad mood, and I was taking it out on you. Both of you. I'm sorry. Really."

Jase is finding it hard to keep a straight face, because he can see Lucy, behind the driving wheel, grinning cheekily, pointing at Alun, and making finger-in-fist signals, indicating that overnight, his father has managed to find someone to clean his pipes out. "That's okay, Dad. No harm done, like."

"No, but seriously, son. I'm sorry."

"Yeah, whatever." Jase pats him on the shoulder. "Come on, old man. Let's get you back to Wales before the wind changes, and you're stuck like this."

CHAPTER SEVEN

"Got those broken window blues? Well, we've all been there. Why not call Indigo Glassworks on [cue number] for all your glazing needs. For aluminium and uPVC windows, doors and conservatories. Don't be blue. Call Indigo, for a free estimate. That number again…"

Jase's expression is glum. "Right. And what you need from me is…"

"We're looking for a slow blues. Up until the first 'Indigo'. Then, you pick things up."

"Pick things up how?"

Tim's smile does not waver. He is accustomed to dealing with artists who are above this kind of thing. "Faster, happier. Sort of a 'Duelling Banjos' vibe."

"But 'Duelling Banjos' is more bluegrass."

"I didn't say 'Duelling Banjos'. I said a 'Duelling Banjos' vibe. If you play 'Duelling Banjos', we'll have to pay the people who wrote 'Duelling Banjos'. If you play something in, say, a country blues style, with a 'Duelling Banjos' vibe, we only have to pay you. Okay?"

"I get you."

Jase wishes Sonia were here. She was the one who got him into this mess. But she's working, elsewhere. And why is he thinking of it as a mess? He's in an actual recording studio, with professional producers, for the first time in his life. He's wearing hi-tech headphones, and sitting in a sci-fi glass booth. He should be leaping around like a hyperactive rabbit, bouncing off the walls. Metaphorically. But he's apprehensive. Pressure, that's what it is. Mustn't let her down.

Sonia didn't exactly beg Tim to see if he could find something for Jase. It's just that the day after the Barfly gig, he'd remarked that he'd look out for opportunities to use him. Maybe in a radio commercial. And it had been a several weeks before Sonia gently reminded him of this. And a few more before he came up with something. Which Jase refused to countenance.

"A debt consolidation company? No fucking way!" Having had to live through his mother's experiences with such people. And more than once having to go, begging-bowl in hand, to a sneering Alun.

But Sonia slightly over-dramatised the embarrassment factor of begging her boss to find work for her boyfriend, and Jase remarked that he'd never asked her to do any such thing, and they had their first proper row, with screaming and everything. But Jase is painfully conscious of the fact that while his girlfriend is a high-flying trainee graphic designer with a nationally renowned advertising agency, he is basically a part-time delivery driver who makes a little money on the side playing in a pub blues band, and still lives with his Mam. And while a single recording session won't iron out the financial discrepancy, it will at least show her that he's willing to make the effort. Thus, a fortnight or so later, when she enquires as to whether he has any ideological objections to the transparent wall installation business, he finds himself painted into a very small corner.

"Just jam for a bit", suggests the affable, corpulent engineer, who's worked with them all, in his time. "Get some mournful riffs down, then some cheerful ones, and we'll do the technical stuff."

"Jam, eh?" Jase has spent the best part of a decade doing little else. And things seem to be going well for the next hour, or so. Until Mr Indigo Glassworks pops in, to see how things are going.

Jase knows the type. The piggy-eyed, thick-as-shit tradesman in a knock-off designer suit, who's lucked into a goldmine and now considers himself to be of the ruling classes. "Is that him?", he asks Tim. "Doesn't look like much." Before Tim has time to turn off the talkback mic.

Jase and the engineer adjourn to share a joint in the toilet, as Tim explains to Mr Indigo the cost implications of Jase's playing anything that sounds too much like "Duelling Fucking Banjos!". The engineer has never seen Ofnadwy Bluesville, but he's heard good things, and he remembers seeing Alun sing, years ago, backed by Marto Cavanaugh, who had, in terms of economy and effectiveness, one of the best live keyboard set-ups he'd ever seen. "Plus, he could play a bit too, like."

"Listen – sorry if I'm being a bit… you know."

"Arsey?"

"I was going to say amateurish."

The engineer breaks into a spluttering laugh, and Jase cannot help but join him. On recovering, he explains that he's seen Oscar-worthy actors reduced to abject, childish pleading in the booth. "I mean, even Bobby De Niro'd have difficulty putting himself in the mind of a friggin' photo-copier."

Back in the studio, Jase does pretty much what he's been doing before, and Mr Indigo declares himself pleased that the boy has followed his instructions. Instructions which, it goes without saying, Tim hasn't deemed worthy of relaying to him.

The session completed, Tim takes Jase for a lunchtime drink. He looks at the young guitar genius through narrowed eyes. "Have you done something to your hair since we last met?" And before he can answer. "Things going well with our Sonia, then?"

"Yeah. Pretty good, I think. She's… you know. Special."

"Well, you're definitely an improvement on the last one." Tim met Michael once or twice. Jase is careful not to seem over-inquisitive. "It's not that he didn't seem like a decent lad. It's just… he didn't speak to her with respect. That's always a sign that you're going to get dumped. Well, either that, or get married." He chuckles, and sighs. "And she was obviously in love with him. Gets you right there". Pointing to his battered heart.

"Do you reckon she's in love with me?"

"Oh, yes. No two ways about it. It's just…" He takes a pensive sip of his vodka and grapefruit-juice. "It's the difference between the way a dog loves its master, and the way a human being loves another human being. You've helped her to grow up."

Jase gulps. "I've never been accused of that before."

That night is the first time Sonia returns to her flat to be greeted by the smell of Jase's patented spicy pasta sauce.

"What have I done to deserve this?"

"It's because of you that I can afford to put wine in it."

She wraps her tired arms around him. "So? Good day? Tim said you took to being a corporate whore like a duck to water."

"An unprofessional duck. Who's prone to seasickness."

"But you never want to do it again?"

Jase shrugs. He's shaken hands with Tim. He's now on his list. Surely this is what being a pro is all about, he muses, cynically.

But the first time the new ad for Indigo Glassworks comes on the radio, while he's sitting at breakfast with his mother, his glee is naive and unmistakable.

While restaurants, art exhibitions, and films are not a problem, it takes a good while before a music act turns up in town which Jase and Sonia feel they can both attend without feeling that they are doing one another a favour. The guilty party is a cultish African-American jazz singer-guitarist, who plays Cardiff's Welsh Club as part of an extensive series of small European dates signalling his comeback from unspecified "health problems". Watching him being interviewed on television a few days earlier, though, on the day of his first show, in London, Jase recognises the "I've seen things you wouldn't believe" expression of the determinedly recovering addict.

There is no support act, only a mix-tape featuring female singers of a sombre/earnest stripe – Aretha Franklin, Francois Hardy, Laura Nyro, Astrud

Gilberto, Aimee Mann. Jase jokes that he can feel his period coming on. Looking around the packed hall, they see a number of faces familiar from local television and the Cardiff music scene. "Just as well I went to the toilet before we came out", quips Sonia, as she makes for the bar.

As Jase is wondering what to do with his empty lager-bottle, he notices that someone has sidled up to him. "Hi – you're that blues guy, aren't you?"

Jase recognises the young man, but tries not to make it too obvious. "Well, I'm a blues guy. Kind of. Hi, there."

"So, is this more your kind of thing, then?"

"No, everything's my kind of thing. It's just... if someone like him's playing in South Wales, you can't not come, can you? It'd just be... rude, like."

They chat casually about guitar-players for a few minutes, until Sonia returns, and gasps, "Bloody hell! It's you!"

"Well, can't argue with that."

The young man is named Gavin, and he is the undeniably charismatic lead singer and guitarist of Cherry Gravy, a band from Mid-Wales who, after several years of toiling away on the Welsh-language music scene, sacked their founder member, hired a style advisor and a turn-tablist, and started singing in English, whereupon they were signed up by a major record-label, and recorded a critically-lauded album of spiky, anthemic pop-rock which eventually went gold, selling particularly well in Scandinavia.

Jase does the formal introductions. "Jason Hopkins; my girlfriend Sonia."

"Gavin", says Gavin, shaking hands.

"I know!" says Sonia. "You're in that band!"

"Sonia – baby – you're totally blowing my cool." Jase smiles apologetically at Gavin. "She doesn't get to meet many international rock stars."

"We met Chattanooga Charlie. But then he died."

"That must have been very nice for you. Well, except the last bit." He turns to Jase. "Listen, erm… why don't you let me have your phone number? There's something I want to talk to you about."

"No problem." Jase writes his number on a beer-mat, and hands it to Gavin.

"Cheers. Well – see you around."

When Gavin is safely back with his gang of inappropriately-dressed friends, Sonia starts to jump up and down. "Cherry Gravy, that's it! I forgot."

"I didn't realise you were familiar with their work."

"Well, I'm not. Not really. But they're always on MTV. You know, that video with the robot baby and the woman with the three bosoms? What do you think he wants to talk to you about?"

Jase has a vague idea. "No idea. Maybe he wants some hints on guitar-playing."

Sonia is just about to venture some speculations of her own when the tape fades down, and the main attraction wanders on stage in a kaftan and dark glasses, strolls up to the microphone, guitar in hand and, without ceremony, launches into his biggest hit. There then follows an hour and a half of songs old and new, jazz classics interspersed with originals, the trademark silky baritone underpinned by lightning-fast arpeggiation. Sonia stands there, open-mouthed, in common with the bulk of the audience, while Jase swears to himself that once and for all he must conquer his puritanical attitude towards using anything other than the standard tuning, and get to grips with the whole jazz chords thing. When the show ends, the acclaim is deafening, drowning out the mix-tape which has been cranked up again, and it does not subside for several minutes, forcing the star to return to the stage. He seems genuinely moved and raises his hands to quieten things down.

"Ladies and gentlemen, thank-you so much. You really don't know how much this means to me." His voice starts to crack with emotion. "I'm gonna do one more song, then, please, please, I sorely need my beauty sleep!"

As the tell-tale opening chords to Elvis Costello's "Almost Blue" start to ring out, Jase and Sonia look at one another. There follows a rendition displaying such artless pathos that not a heart in the room remains unmelted. "Right", thinks Jase, "I'm never letting my dad murder that song ever again."

As they walk back to Sonia's flat, their head are too full of the wonders they have just beheld for them to brood overmuch in respect of the Cherry Gravy incident. In fact, it is not until his phone rings when he is on the train back to the Valleys in mid-morning, that Gavin re-enters his consciousness.

"Hi, Jason?"

"Yes?"

"It's me. Gavin. From last night?"

"Oh, yeah. Wow. How are you? Amazing gig."

"Yeah, wondrous stuff. Listen, erm… can you talk?"

"Erm… yeah."

"Okay – it's like this…"

Jase calls an emergency band meeting in the pub that evening. Item one is his autocratic "Almost Blue" decision, accompanied by an explanation. No-one is especially disappointed; Lucy, at whose instigation it was added to the set in the first place is so in love with the original (and with Elvis Costello), that it always seemed like a sacrilege, and Alun isn't a fan of the high notes.

"Okay. Item two. I've been invited to play guitar with Cherry Gravy on their UK tour, which starts in a fortnight's time. Should I do it, or what?"

Understandably, it's a while before everyone takes this in. Lucy is the first to speak.

"Cherry Gravy? *The* Cherry Gravy?"

Dai seems put out. "I didn't know you knew them." They are associates of the band of which he was briefly a member.

Jase explains the circumstances of his meeting with Gavin. "I mean, I'd heard they were looking to make changes." Having released the second album, which has, so far, sold disappointingly.

Alun sits back in his seat, and takes a long sip of bitter. "You seem very calm about this, son."

"Calm?"

"You're being asked to join a successful band. Major label, touring commitments."

"I'm not being asked to join. I'd be an employee."

"For the time being. You don't seem very excited."

"I'm not a big fan."

"I'm not a big fan of… the Welsh National Opera, but if they asked me around for a sing-along, I'd be dead chuffed." His eyes narrow. "What does Sonia think?"

"She doesn't know."

"Ah." Alun nods, wisely. "You haven't asked her permission yet."

"I don't need to ask her permission. I need to ask your permission. As my fellow band members."

"And if we say yes?", wonders Lucy.

"I'll have to tell her."

"Tell her about the offer?" Dai winks at the other two. "Or tell her you're going?"

"We'll cross that bridge when we come to it." Jase pulls out a copy of Ofnadwy Bluesville's latest itinerary. "Now, we've got four gigs in those three weeks: Cardiff twice, Stoke and Oxford. I've already checked – the Cardiff ones we can do anytime, the Stoke one we can reschedule, but Oxford's a festival, so… "

"You've already checked?"

"Yes, Dad. Checked. As opposed to cancelling them, breaking up the band and running away to become a pop star."

"So – how much they paying you, then?", asks Dai.

Jase tells them. A silence ensues. Alun gets up, goes to the bar and orders a double-whisky, which he drinks on the spot, before returning to the table.

"Erm… run that by me again, son?"

Jase repeats the figure. "I mean, it's not even confirmed yet, I… I've got to meet the band, the others might not like me, I… I've got to learn the songs…"

"*How* much?!", asks Dai, not entirely convinced that he isn't lying, off his tits, in a ditch somewhere, imagining all this.

"A lot", replies Lucy. "Hey – Jase – have I ever told you that I love you? I've just added you to my list of blokes I'd turn for." The others being Costello, Woody Allen, Isaac Hayes, and Michael Madsen, a.k.a. Mr Blond from "Reservoir Dogs".

"So – what do you reckon?"

Alun looks at the others. "Jason – did you really think we were going to tell you you couldn't go?" An evil grin. "Frankly, I think we're the least of your worries."

"*How* much?!", asks Sonia, as they meet for lunch the next day.

"Enough so I'll be able to hold my end up in this relationship. For a couple of months, anyway."

"Oh." She looks down at the checkerboard tablecloth. "This is my fault, isn't it? Making you feel self-conscious about not earning much money."

Jase reaches over and envelops her hand in his. "I want to be a professional musician, Sonia. It's the only thing I'm half good at. Well, the only thing I'm prepared to do in public."

"Don't flatter yourself." Sonia sighs. "So, is it all sex and drugs with these guys? 'Hammer Of The Gods' stuff?" Jase raises his eyebrows. "Michael was a big Led Zeppelin fan. It was his favourite book."

"Look – nothing like that's going to happen. Not with me, anyway. What we've got's too important."

"I've heard that before."

"Anyone would think you didn't trust me."

"You, I trust." She reaches under the table and grasps the tip of his penis between her thumb and forefinger, making him wince. "Little Jason, I'm not so sure about."

Jase wriggles free. "Look – it's not a done deal, anyway. I'm only telling you just in case. Not telling you. Asking you. Well, telling you, so I can ask you." He senses her conflicting emotions. "Look – if you say don't want me to go for it, I won't. It's not a big deal. I mean, can you name the bloke who plays second guitar for the Stereophonics? Or The Manic Street Preachers' keyboard-player? It's not like it's my big shot at stardom or anything. It's just a job."

Not that Jase feels as though he's walking into a job interview when he arrives at Cherry Gravy's rehearsal studio shortly before six that evening. Although he's never had many job interviews so, in all honesty, it's hard to say. Gavin greets him with a warm handshake. Rhys the drummer, and the other Rhys on bass are more cagey. The decks-man is nowhere to be seen. "DJ Dwm is no longer a member of the group", explains Gavin.

"We're going for a more organic sound, like", says Rhys the Bass.

"Back to our roots, innit", adds Rhys the Beat.

That morning's post included a budget MP3 player with both Cherry Gravy albums saved onto it, and Jase has spent every spare moment listening to it, having been embarrassed when, on the phone the previous day, Gavin had asked how well he knew their stuff.

"Oh. W-well, that's okay – we're looking for a fresh perspective, anyway."

Jase plugs in his trusty axe, and as they start up one of their airplay hits, he stands there listening before contributing some fills, then some background rhythm guitar. Gavin brings things to a halt, as they approach the third chorus, and asks Jase if he can try and stick a solo in there, where the ragtime sample kicks in on the original record. Jase promises to oblige, and they start again. At the end, Rhys and Rhys exchange positive-vibe glances, and Gavin smiles. "Was that alright, like?" Jase would rather hear verbal confirmation, since he's never been that confident about picking up interpersonal signals. Although his skills in that area have improved somewhat since he's been with Sonia.

"That was fine, Jase. Better than fine. Guys?"

Rhys and Rhys confirm their approval, in Welsh. Instinctively, Jase takes the tactical decision to conceal the fact that he can understand virtually every word they're saying – he studied Welsh at A-level, but he's not a fluent speaker of the Cymraeg. "Sorry?"

He gets the thumbs up, and without warning, they launch into one of their newer songs. Jase is quicker off the mark this time, augmenting Gavin's guitar-work from early in verse one, and providing a brief solo, unbidden. He messes up the ending, though. "Too many notes, court composer", jokes Rhys the Beat.

"Er, Jase?" Gavin reaches into his pocket and takes out a fiver. "You couldn't pop down the offy on the corner and bring us a four-pack? Anything'll do, as long as it's ice-cold."

"No problem."

Once outside, Jase dawdles, painfully aware of how time flies during band meetings, and wanting to give them enough time to complete their deliberations. In the off-licence, as well as the four cans of Brains Dark, he picks up a half-litre of cherry cola, to deal with the dryness in his throat, drinking it all down in one go, such that when he returns to the rehearsal room, to be met by cries of "Nice one, mate!" and "You're in!", he lets out an enormous burp which echoes creepily off the walls.

"I mean, cheers, guys. I won't let you down."

After they've seen off the cans, it's round to the local for more beer and male bonding. He notices that Rhys and the other Rhys in particular look somewhat older than they do on their videos, but why the hell not? It's not as though they sing songs about walking girls home from school, or being neurotic about their virginity. Oh no, wait, they do. Or, rather, that was the first album. The new one deals with the state of the earth – war, poverty, greenhouse gases, that kind of thing. And fair enough – in the early days, they played more benefit gigs than paid ones. They've paid their dues, and were due some good fortune.

"So, Dai Williams is in your band, isn't he?"

"Yeah, that's right."

"Is he still… you know…?"

Jase nods, sadly. Although Dai seems to be coherent more often, these days. But then he doesn't see him every day, the way he used to, before Sonia. "Still, I've been there. I know what it's like, being addicted. Which is why…" He knows he'll have to tiptoe on eggshells here. "I mean… all that on-the-road stuff. Drugs, and that. I'm hoping to avoid… you know. Getting into trouble."

Embarrassed glances all round. "It's up to you, mate."

"Although, frankly, these days, it's a cup of cocoa and a good book, most nights."

"Especially now the record-company's mysteriously stopped throwing money at us."

Several beers later, Jase summons up the courage to wonder how they decided so quickly that he was the man for them.

Rhys the bass puts an arm around his shoulders. "You can play your instrument, and you appear not to be an arsehole. Quite frankly, given the people we've been looking at, you're over-qualified.

"Can I ask you a question?" Gavin is the most coherent of the lot of them, having switched to alco-pops early in the evening. "Do you want to be a star?"

"Erm… not really. I want to make a living doing something I enjoy doing. Like most people."

Gavin gives him a slow hand-clap. "Right answer." He leans in. "Now, tell me the truth."

"The truth is…" Jase feels his innards sink, as they always do when he's being sincere whilst intoxicated. "I'm not star material. Look at my face – is this the face of a star?"

"Yeah, you're an ugly bastard, right enough", says Rhys the Beat.

"I just want to be something other than a waste of space for the first time in my life."

A waste of space is exactly what Jase is when he rolls up at Sonia's, round about midnight. "I got the gig, love", he gurgles, before passing out on her sofa. He joins her in bed at four in the morning, having been sick in the toilet, and passes out once more. He comes to around ten, and finds himself alone, a note pinned to the unoccupied pillow next to him. "Drunken tosser. See you for lunch? Love, S."

He spends the rest of the morning drinking coffee, bringing it up again, and making phone-calls. By lunchtime, he feels sufficiently strong to face solids, and orders the all-day student breakfast, while Sonia gets the cheese salad. She examines the concert dates with interest. "London, Glasgow, Leeds, Newcastle, Aberdeen, Birmingham, Bristol, Norwich, Plymouth, Liverpool, Brighton, Manchester, London." Drawing the route-map in the air with her index-finger. "Who booked this tour? Jackson Pollock?"

"I get the feeling they had to take what was available at relatively short notice." With a mouth full of bacon and beans.

"You don't say. Still…" An idea begins to form in her head. "At least you get a day off between Aberdeen and Birmingham."

"Yeah. The boys thought we might chill a bit, in the Highlands. Get in touch with our Celtic roots, kind of thing."

"Birmingham's only twenty minutes from Wolverhampton. On the train."

"Oh, yeah?"

"You know? Wolverhampton? Where my parents live?"

Jase's masticating ceases. "Your parents?"

"I mean, I've met yours." Alun, obviously. Violet on the infrequent weekends when she's gone up to stay in Jase's bedroom, with the patches of oblong paleness on the wall where his posters of naked ladies were, until very recently; stilted conversation about the soaps and the weather; eating meals of mash and dry chops, followed by tinned peaches, washed down with raspberry pop. "It'd be nice."

Jase smiles. "Yeah. 'Oh, hiya, Mr and Mrs Raymond. My name's Jason. I'm the semi-professional guitar-player and former drug-addict who's shagging your daughter. Can I stash these bags somewhere while I go down the pub?'"

"It's a Saturday, too. I won't have to take too many days off work. It'll be... nice." Hoping that repetition will make it true.

"What have you told them about me?"

Sonia starts to squirm. "Well, they know you exist."

"Oh. Well, they're already an improvement on my dad." He chuckles. He looks at her. "Look – do you really want me to meet them?"

"I... I... I..."

Jase puts a hand on hers. "You've got a couple of weeks to think about it, love. I'm leaving it entirely up to you." He sniggers inwardly, knowing how much she hates it when he puts pressure on her, while loving it the other way round.

CHAPTER EIGHT

There is a week of rehearsals prior to the tour. Late morning till early evening in the studio, then out to the pub with the lads, then back to Sonia's. It isn't till Thursday, after Jase has come in relatively sober, and they both nod off in front of a nature documentary, with the remains of a takeaway on the table in front of them, that it dawns on them that they appear to be living together, and surviving the experience. But on Saturday, Jase is back off home to pack, and see his Mam, and meet up with the rest of the Ofnadwy Bluesville for a curiously subdued drink at the Unaffiliated. And on Sunday morning, it's time to meet up with the boys from Cherry Gravy. "Relax, Jase", says Gavin, noting his apprehension. "It's going to be a marvellous adventure."

That night's first London gig is nerve-wracking fun, if not particularly well-attended. "It might have been nice if someone from the record company had turned up," grumbles Rhys the Beat, in the dressing-room, afterwards. But someone has – only he leaves before they come on, because his more immediate concern is the support band, Hammerfight, a trio of black-clad seventeen-year-olds from Cornwall. They've been signed up in order to appeal to fans of kiddie-pop who turn to the dark side come puberty, and they keep themselves to themselves. They only play a twenty-minute set, consisting of around a dozen songs, in a Gothic speed-metal vein. Jase quite likes them, feeling that they were the kind of band John Peel would have adored, but the other three are disdainful. After the record company man has put Hammerfight to bed, he comes out with their label-mates Cherry Gravy, taking them to a club, and distributing pills. Jase takes his first E since he was fifteen, knowing that he'll hate himself in the morning, not for endangering his brain, but for dancing like a learning-disabled wallaby to music he despises. And so it proves.

It is not until they are well into the drive to Glasgow the next morning that Jase enquires as to the whereabouts of Hammerfight, and is told that they have taken the 'plane.

"You what?!"

Rhys the Beat's much older brother, Huw, is the driver. "Their mums and dads made the record company promise. They're the ones who had to sign the contract, see, so they were calling the shots, like."

"So how long's this trip taking us ordinary mortals?"

"Only another six hours to go. If we don't hit any of the rush-hours. They've done us proud with this baby, though." He pats the dashboard of Cherry Gravy's minibus, bought when the company was still in love with them. "Seen us through thick and thin, this has." Jase makes a mental note of the time and date, ready for the inevitable breakdown.

They arrive in Glasgow in early evening, to find that Hammerfight have already done their sound-check, and are busy signing autographs for schoolgirls on the steps of the venue. "Coming tonight, girls?", asks Gavin, cheekily, to be met by insolent, dismissive glances. "I only asked."

The hall, three-quarters full for Hammerfight, is half empty by the time the Gravy come on, but those who are there seem to have a jolly time. A group of fans take them out for after-hours drinks, and Rhys the Bass goes home with a ginger-dreadlocked fat lass.

Hammerfight's flight to Leeds is hit by turbulence, and they ask their record company girl to organise road transport for them from here on in. Arriving late, they deign to talk unprompted to Cherry Gravy for the first time, and after the gig, they slip the leash and let the older crew take them out on the piss. Several years of exposure to scrumpy, however, have given them iron constitutions, and they drink the Welsh contingent quite literally under the table.

Able to afford a late start, the bands drive in convoy to Newcastle, where they spend the day drinking and shopping for records. Jase argues good-naturedly with Hammerfight's guitarist about axe-heroes, but they manage to agree on Hendrix and Johnny Marr, and the younger axe-man buys a Neil Young compilation, in return for Jase buying a Frank Zappa one. The gig that night follows the same pattern as before, with a set of young fans being replaced during the interval with a smaller group of older, more colourfully dressed ones. This starts to rankle with Gavin, who repairs sulkily to his boarding-house bedroom when the rest of them go out to play.

The tedium of the drive to Aberdeen is broken when Cherry Gravy's mini-bus breaks down (four days, three hours and thirteen minutes, notes Jase.) They make a mobile-call to Hammerfight's camper-van which proves, being two years newer and a few thousand quid more plush, well able to accommodate both bands. As well as the fifteen-year-old groupie that Hammerfight picked up in Geordieland. There is then an unscheduled stop in Edinburgh while Rhys the Bass, who is a trained social worker, shepherds her into Waverly Station, and onto the train back home.

In the dressing-room, after the Aberdeen gig, when once more Hammerfight fans outnumber those of Cherry Gravy, Gavin finally blows his top. "Thousand-seater venues? We should be fucking storming thousand-seater venues! On our own! We shouldn't be playing second fucking fiddle to a bunch of fucking kids!"

Jase keeps his opinions to himself, and goes to bed early.

In the morning, he bids a temporary farewell to his fellow rockers, who have arranged a day of artificial-slope snow-boarding, and commences the ludicrously lengthy train-journey to Wolverhampton.

During the longest stretch, from Edinburgh to Birmingham, Jase manages to finally complete the Marlon Brando autobiography that he was given for his twenty-first birthday. Between Birmingham and Wolverhampton, he is forced to stand, and finds himself pondering the nature of greatness. As light relief from pondering the nature of his girlfriend's parents.

His heart leaps as he sees that Sonia is waiting for him on the platform. She kisses him extravagantly as he disembarks, the couple jostled by inconsiderate home-coming commuters. "I've missed you so much."

The car is unfamiliar. "My Dad's", says Sonia.

"Oh." Jase feels deflated as he climbs in. "Does that mean it'd be inappropriate to stop somewhere for a quickie in the back seat?"

Sonia takes her seat at the wheel, and slips a hand between Jase's legs. "Has little Jason been behaving himself?"

"Pretty much." Jase has been comforting himself using boarding-house toilet tissue when appropriate. "How's little Sonia?"

"Hungry", she says, "Looking forward to her Friday night feast."

"Great. What time do we eat?"

"Okay – I think we're slightly over-doing this metaphor."

"What metaphor? I've only had a cheese roll all day!"

Sonia's parent's house is not far from the city-centre. Jase is strangely reassured by the greyness, and the narrow terraced streets. "Yes, Jason – I admit it – I'm working-class."

As the car pulls up outside the door, it opens, and Mrs Raymond is standing there. Jase can immediately see where Sonia got her posterior from, but the face is open and friendly. "You must be Jason. Dorothy. Pleased to meet you." Jase realises that he was expecting, for some reason, a West Indian accent, but she is pure Midlands.

He hands her the box of shortbread he bought in Aberdeen. "Fresh from Scotland. Well, probably not that fresh, like, but you know what I mean."

Sonia's father is short, and balding, but still looks younger than Alun, although he's four or five years older. The handshake is warm, but the look is suspicious. Jase hands Cliff the half-bottle of Scotch purchased from the same shop as the shortbread. "Only a half?"

"I… well, I didn't want you to think I thought you were some kind of alcoholic, or something, like." The smell of spicy chicken is making his intestines perform somersaults. But first must come the inquisition.

Yes, he is does enjoy being a professional musician; yes, he does envisage it being a part of his life into the foreseeable future, even if he doesn't make big money out of it; no, he can't read music well enough to do the classical thing; yes, he was once a heroin user, but he never injected, and he's now as clean as clean can be; no, he hasn't been to university; yes, he'd like to, at some point; no, school-teaching doesn't feel as though it could be an option at the moment; no, he's not religious, but there must be something in it, which explains all these bloody wars; yes, he is in love with their daughter; no, he doesn't know what the future holds for them, what with him coming from a broken home, and Sonia being exposed to successful businessmen every day of the week; yes, he would like some hot pepper sauce, thank-you very much.

By this time they're at dinner, and Jase is devouring his chicken and red beans and rice with some enthusiasm. "This is lovely."

"Well, it's not as good as my Mum's." Cliff is touchingly modest. "But that was authentic Jamaican. This is the Wolverhampton version."

Cliff does all the cooking these days, since he went part-time at work. He's a psychiatric nurse, and he was attacked a year or so ago by a schizophrenic patient wielding a glass ashtray. Not seriously injured, but it badly affected his confidence, and anyway, there's no need for both of them to work every day that God sends, now the kids are out of the house and both working (Sonia's older brother, Carl, being a policeman in Birmingham). Dorothy is also a nurse, but works on a paediatric ward, where the chances of being physically attacked are more remote, "but it certainly messes with your emotions".

They don't usually serve wine at dinner, but since they've got company, Dorothy has cracked open a bottle of Soave. Cliff doesn't have any, since he needs to get ready for work – he does three nights a week – and Jase chooses to remain alcohol-free, for fear of embarrassing himself whilst excessively at ease.

As Cliff takes his leave, his half-cut wife and daughter are lounging around the front-room, singing along to Motown songs, while the pale Welsh youth accompanies them on his unplugged guitar. "Er, I probably won't see you tomorrow, Jason, so… all the best."

"Thanks, Mr Raymond. Erm… it was a pleasure to meet you."

Sonia's father does not reply, but there is nothing malevolent in his smile, which Jase takes as a good sign.

Dorothy staggers up to bed around ten, and Sonia immediately seduces Jase on the sofa. "So, do you think they like me?", he wonders, breathless, afterwards.

"They like you as a person." Sonia ponders. "Maybe not as a boyfriend for me, but that's really not their concern."

They finish the wine, and Jase talks about life on tour. It still feels somewhat like an adventure, as Gavin had promised, but from here on in it's going to be a bit of a slog. And he's discovered that the travel sickness which he suffered from as a child might not have been entirely conquered.

Sonia puts him to bed in Carl's old room – controversially, in these parts, a shrine to Aston Villa F.C. She refuses to sleep with him in there, because it would just feel wrong, and her own bedroom is adjacent to her parents', so *that* isn't about to happen. Jase doesn't mind too much – she's already eased his tension, and the mattress is the softest he's experienced for some days. He goes to sleep quickly, and dreams of black-clad dwarves with Cornish accents doing a Maypole dance around him.

In the morning, he is awakened by someone tickling his scrotum. Mercifully, it is Sonia. "We've got a window! Mum's just gone to work, and Dad won't be back till ten!" They repair to her bedroom. Jase is surprised to discover the walls hung not with posters of hunky male film and pop stars, but large-format pencil-drawings of same. Post-coitus, he sits up and asks her to talk him through her oeuvre.

"Charles Bronson? I didn't know you were a Bronson fan."

"I'm not. He just had a fascinating face."

"I've got a fascinating face. You should do a drawing of me."

"How do you know I haven't?"

"Ah." Jase nods, sagely. "You've tried, but you keep throwing them away, because you can't find a way of making me look beautiful."

"You're the most beautiful person in the world", insists Sonia. "It's just... difficult to interpret your inner charm in visual terms."

"In other words, I look like a troll."

"Yep."

They get up and have toast and tea for breakfast. Then, Sonia puts Jase's washing in the machine, before taking him on a walking tour of the sights of Wolverhampton, including the art gallery, her old school, and the back alley where she let Rizwan Sherwani feel under her bra when they were thirteen. "He wasn't impressed."

When they get back to the house, Cliff's things are in the hallway, indicating that he is back from work, but has gone to bed. They finish Jase's laundry, pack up his things, and drive to Birmingham so that Sonia can show him the Bullring. An hour into vaguely tedious couply shopping, Jase is shocked to spot a familiar gaggle of humanity mooching around HMV's rock section. It is Hammerfight, with Rhys and the other Rhys their unlikely chaperones. "Bloody hell – what are you guys doing here?"

It transpires that during the previous day's snowboarding, the members of Hammerfight made a habit of using their older but less experienced colleagues in Cherry Gravy as slalom poles. One of them (they are unclear as to which), missed Gavin by scant millimetres, whereupon he utterly mislaid the plot, and stormed off, seeking refuge in the nearest bar. On the drive back to the boarding-house, he was monosyllabic, and when the group went for drinks in a nearby student pub, he joined them late, and proceeded to badmouth the Hammerfight lads, bitterly condemning his bandmates as "bradwyr" (traitors) when they defended them. He then went off drinking by himself. As the evening wore on, the remaining musos began to balk at the prospect of the four-hundred-odd mile drive to Birmingham starting at seven the next morning. Rhys and Rhys dared Hammerfight to phone up their record company contact demanding that their private jet be reinstated, for them and their friends Cherry Gravy. Within the half-hour, the return call came, regretting that this was impossible at such short notice, but informing them that flights had been booked for the six of them from Aberdeen International Airport the following morning. Shocked into sobriety, they rushed back to their lodgings, and told Gavin the good news. He was having none of it, though, refusing to accept the patronage of these upstarts. The following morning, when they tried to persuade him once more, he remained emphatically obstinate, saying that he would drive. Thus, Huw took his place on the 'plane, and Rhys the Bass, Rhys the Beat and Hammerfight arrived in town in good time for a pub lunch and a spot of record-shopping. They estimate that Gavin should just about have crossed the border by now, but he isn't answering his mobile.

Deducing that she will get no more sense from Jase now that he's found his little friends, Sonia bids him a fond farewell, promising to see him later. There is much laddish guitar talk, and an afternoon drink, before they check in at their boarding-house.

Gavin contrives to turn up at the Birmingham venue fifteen minutes before Cherry Gravy are due on, although the band have been made aware, in a phone-call from a music-loving fellow guest, that he arrived at their lodgings shortly after they left for the soundcheck. The gig follows the usual pattern – a mass of frenzied Hammerfight fans replaced at half-time by a more selective sample of level-headed Gravy devotees. Jase is easily able to spot Sonia, swaying near the front, accompanied by a young black man who, despite being twice her height, with better hair, is the dead spit of her.

"Jason, Carl; Carl, Jason". They shake hands as Sonia introduces them at the bar. He has decided not to invite them backstage, because of the atmosphere being (a) frosty and (b) full of illicit smoke.

"Nice to meet you."

"I see what you mean about the audience." Sonia has been kept up to date on happenings, during Jase's nightly calls. "Talk about oil and water."

"Don't suppose either band's your kind of thing, eh, Carl?" Jase doesn't feel as nervous as he thought he might do, meeting his girlfriend's brother, the giant black policeman.

"I can always appreciate good musicianship." Carl displays the diplomacy which stands him in good stead on the mean streets of the Second City.

They chat about nothing much for twenty minutes or so, then Carl pops to the toilet. "Ooh – he doesn't like you at all." Jase examines Sonia's expression, and finds her not to be joking.

"Oh." Disappointed.

"No, that's a good thing. He loved Michael."

"Ah."

Sonia makes it clear that she would welcome the opportunity to pay a visit to Jase's room, bearing in mind that they won't be able to get together again for at least another week. Jase is sharing with Gavin, however. "Damn!"

Carl returns. "Coming, then, Tich-face?"

Sonia whacks her brother on the arm, and Jase cannot hold in a spluttering laugh. "I'll have to start calling you that!"

"Not if you like being attached to your testicles", she growls into his ear.

"You're not joining us for Sunday lunch, then", enquires Carl, in an orderly fashion.

"Nah. We've got to get down to Bristol. Give your mum and dad my best, though?"

"Will do." Carl stands by patiently as the lovers kiss goodbye.

They both look back at Jase as they reach the door of the now-deserted hall, Sonia with longing, Carl with suspicion. But Jase is painfully aware that he has always been, for some unaccountable reason, an acquired taste, even within his own family.

On returning to the dressing-room, Cherry Gravy are sitting around, uncommunicative. Hammerfight are elsewhere, having been taken clubbing by a cohort of their pubescent acolytes. Rhys and Rhys were tempted to join them, but discouraged by one of Gavin's fiery glares.

"Fuck it – I'm going out." Rhys the Beat leaves, followed by Huw, and Rhys the Bass.

Gavin gives Jase a baleful look. "Go ahead. I'm not stopping you."

"Actually, I'm a bit knackered."

"Oh. Alright." He sighs, and pulls on his jacket. "Fancy a walk?"

It's a half-hour trek back to the boarding house, and Jase feels privileged to be party to the untold story of Cherry Gravy: Gavin, Rhys, Rhys and original guitarist-songwriter, Bryn, meeting on the first day of secondary school and playing their debut gig at a Christmas assembly; the years of honing their craft; the dozens of experimental recordings before making their first independent single; the long period as the reliable support act to a thousand less aesthetically subtle outfits on the Welsh-language touring circuit. There are good times, of course – the girls, the video-shoots, the girls, the parties, the girls, the intense interviews with student newspapers, the girls. And just when they're approaching thirty, and starting to think about calling it a day and fading into the background, they get the approach from the record company. Drop the Welsh-language thing, or at least save it for B-sides, smarten up your image, and you've got a deal. And Bryn objects. Less to do with the language issue, than with the concept of leaping into bed with a multi-national which has links with the arms industry. The others point out that tobacco kills more people every year than war, and refer to his sixty-a-day cigarette habit, and the several thousand quid which he therefore donates annually to the cause. Plus, they'd quite like to be able to buy houses, and that. They come to an agreement: he gives them a handful of the songs that he wrote for a boy-band musical which was abandoned, and ceases to be a member of the group. These tunes, duly rocked up and anglicised, form the basis of the hit album. Cherry Gravy get famous and criticised for selling out; Bryn earns a good chunk of the royalties, and kudos for standing by his principles - everybody's happy. Until album two, which Gavin, Rhys and Rhys have to write themselves. And which, by most considered estimates, is shite.

Jase does not make the obvious suggestion – that they ask their former band-mate to write some more songs for them. He is well aware that Bryn has blossomed into a successful solo-artist in the electro-folk vein, and is constantly on S4C.

"You see, we could survive being shite! Dozens of bands do very well out of being shite! But… but…" This latest indignity, being constantly upstaged by a bunch of inarticulate schoolboys, who've never even bothered to come up with melodies and lyrics in the first place, just shouted slogans, is too much.

"I quite like them." Jase has grown particularly fond of Hammerfight's "The Knowing Laughter of Sexually Confident Ugly Older Women", and "Swearing Is The New Politics, You Fascist Fuckhead". "They're good lads, Gav."

"Yeah, whatever." Gavin lapses into monosyllabicity, and the pair do not communicate in complete sentences until they are both tucked up in their adjacent beds.

"Tell you what, though – I'm definitely reaching the end of my tether."

"What?" Jase is disturbed by his sombre tone. "Hey – don't do anything… you know… stupid, like."

"I'm not a stupid man, Jase. Sweet dreams."

Jase lies awake, worrying, for all of five minutes, before falling asleep, and dreaming of being chased by huge policemen.

At breakfast, Gavin seems like a new man – greeting the Hammerfight boys cordially, laughing and chatting with his fellow Cherry Gravies. The drive to Bristol is uneventful, and they are met by a representative of the record company, who takes both bands out for a meal in an Italian restaurant. Jase notices, however, that attempts by members of Cherry Gravy to talk business with him are ruthlessly stonewalled.

The Bristol gig being the nearest to a hometown show for Cherry Gravy, much of the afternoon is taken up with family reunions. Dai, Lucy and Carol turn up at the pub, along with Violet. It transpires that Alun has nobly forsaken his opportunity to see his only son headlining at a major venue – Violet indicated that she wanted to go, but wouldn't if her hated ex was there. Lucy has brought her camcorder, though, to immortalise the event for his benefit.

"So, what's it like being a proper rock star, then?", wonders Carol, eyes twinkling coquettishly.

He updates her on how it feels to drive from London to Glasgow, in a moribund minibus, with a hangover, in close proximity to four relative strangers who, if you only realised, are mere days away from wanting to kill one another. "So, you might say it's not all glamour."

As he watches Dai chatting animatedly away with old acquaintances Rhys and Rhys, Jase feels a twinge of something which feels dangerously like jealousy.

"I've missed you, mate", he says, a beer or so later.

"It's only been a week, mun, what's up with you?"

"No, I mean… I know we haven't spent much time together since… you know… Sonia."

Dai pats him on the shoulder. "Don't worry about it, son. You've got your lady, I've got mine."

"Anyway", chips in Lucy, "You were only ever mates because nobody else would talk to either of you."

Jase and Dai smile uncomfortably, conscious that this is closer to the mark than she might have supposed.

That night's gig follows the usual format. Lucy is approached by a security guard, who claps a hand on her lens, while she is filming the frenzied response to Hammerfight's aural onslaught. He has been warned by the record-company not to let anyone take any bootleg video footage of the youngsters. The sight of her ostentatiously turning off the camcorder and putting it her bag is not good enough for him, and he demands her tape. Furious, she offers him outside, so they can settle this like men. He backs off in alarm. "Well, alright – you've been warned." And disappears.

There is no such corporate interference when Cherry Gravy come on. "Ooh, I didn't realise it was these!" squeals Violet delightedly, when they play their biggest hit, which was a fixture on local radio a year or so before. Jase is conscious of holding back, not wanting it to look as though he's showing off when the time comes for his solos. Lucy glances over at Dai, and sees tears in his eyes.

After the gig, Gavin quietly packs up his things, puts on his coat, and glances out of the window, to where his wife is waiting at the wheel of their car. "Listen, guys – I've given this a lot of thought. This has been my last show with Cherry Gravy."

As far as Jase is concerned, this is not quite a bolt from the blue. Rhys and Rhys, however, stare in astonishment. "But… but what about the tour?"

"Do what you like. I've had enough humiliation. See you."

And all at once, he is no longer there.

"Look – all he said to me was that he was reaching the end of his rope, like." Jase chooses to stay and take part in the post-mortem. "I thought he might be… you know… suicidal."

"Now, that I could forgive." Rhys the Beat is the very embodiment of the word "saturnine". "At least then we might sell some records."

Rhys the Bass manages to get the record company man on his mobile and delivers the bad news. The record company man is hosting a private party for Hammerfight in his hotel-suite, and doesn't appear to give much of a toss.

"But what are we going to do about the tour?", insists Rhys. He sighs and hangs up. "He'll call us in the morning." It being a Sunday night, and them being strangers in town, they're unable to find anywhere to have a late drink, so it's back to the boarding house for sober recriminations and fitful sleep.

In the morning, the record company man sends a car round to bring the remaining members of Cherry Gravy to his suite for a conference. Jase is loath to join them, but Rhys and Rhys insist: "You're one of us now."

Hammerfight sit around the edges of the room looking like guilty schoolboys, although this is probably attributable more to the brace of partied-out adolescent glamour models seen breakfasting in the hotel dining-room than anxiety at having caused the demise of a major band. It boils down to this: they've already scrapped that night's date in Norwich, and most of the rest of the tour can go, if absolutely necessary, apart from the London show in a week or so's time, for which alternative arrangements can be made. And Plymouth, the next night, which is a big deal – virtually a home-coming gig for the Hammerfight lads; the local media will be in a frenzy. There's not enough time to arrange another band, "so, I was wondering if the three of you could cobble something together?"

It takes Rhys the Beat the longest to work it out. "You... you want us to be *their* support band?"

"It goes without saying, you'll be well remunerated."

Rhys the Beat leaps, furious, to his feet. Thinking as one, Rhys the Bass and Jase follow suit and gently but forcefully steer him into the bathroom, where he throws a few things around. "The impertinence! The fucking impertinence."

But Jase has an idea whereby they can get through this with dignity intact.

Five minutes later, they emerge. Rhys the Bass is their spokesman. "Okay. Let's talk terms."

The word goes out that Cherry Gravy have pulled out of the tour, but that Hammerfight will still be fulfilling their dates. Refunds will be available to Gravy fans at the point of sale, and to make up for the curtailed show, all Hammerfight fans who attend will be given an exclusive, signed two-track CD. After Hammerfight have played, each hall will host a club night, complete with sounds selected by the band, and a chance to meet the boys. The appearance of an untried and unsigned support band goes unheralded.

When Rhys the Bass steps up to the mic in front of the crowd of expectant West Country teenagers on Tuesday night, his nervousness about what is to follow is tempered by mortification at the fact that he has spent much of the previous hour chatting up one of Hammerfight's mothers, unwittingly in the presence of her jovial but immense husband. "Hello", he says. "We are the RRJ Blues Lamentation."

Having taken the plunge by purchasing a bottleneck, and retuning his guitar to an open A configuration, Jase plays a few gentle chords and flourishes, before breaking off and pointing to Rhys the Beat, who ferociously unleashes his best approximation of a high-speed junglist rhythm, to which Rhys the Bass adds some spare, delicate, jazzy lines. Jase stands with his head down, waiting for the spirit to move him. When the moment is right, Jase leaps into the air, and on landing, commences a intense, frenzied, crunching thrash which continues, unrelenting, for a full fifteen minutes, the drumbeat appearing to remain steady, but actually subtly accelerating, and the bass-line intensifying in contrapuntal complexity until they reach the perfect conflation of melody, noise and angst, whereupon Jase raises his fist, to usher in a shattering silence, which he breaks with a painfully brief one-string solo, before the three come together once more in one final, thunderous, apocalyptic chord. The three of them walk off stage without further acknowledgement of the audience. It is not until Hammerfight come bursting into their dressing-room that they realise that the crowd is still applauding, and demanding more.

"They want an encore!"

Rhys the Beat snarls. "The RRJ Blues Lamentation does not do encores."

"Besides which, my fingers are bleeding", adds Rhys the Bass.

The record company consent, with bad grace, to allow the Lamentation to fulfil the remaining tour dates, having been hassled by Hammerfight, who are desperate to see if the oldsters can pull it off again. They can, and do, whipping the crowds in Liverpool, Brighton and Manchester into something vaguely resembling a frenzy - but more confused - prior to Hammerfight's equally brutal, but marginally less nihilistic sets. With Gavin gone, Rhys and Rhys now better understanding Hammerfight's commitment, and the younger crew appreciative of the former Cherry Gravy's professionalism, the remaining after-show parties are resolutely boyish and beerish, any young women who turn up appearing to find the Welshmen too scary to talk to.

On the last night, Jase does not notice the whispered conversations between Rhys the Beat, Rhys the Bass, and the record company contact who has come to ensure that Hammerfight survive long enough to make it to what has now become a high-profile London showcase. Whilst Jase is lecturing Hammerfight's drummer on the subject of his drugs hell, Rhys the Bass unsubtly interposes himself. "Hey, Jase – that guitar of yours must have taken a bit of a battering over the past couple of days."

"Occupational hazard, like." Jase is philosophical.

"How long have you had it? Nine, ten years?"

"Something like that."

"Still, I suppose you'll be able to get a new one, now."

"Er, yeah. The money'll come in really handy, cheers."

"Or you could just spend it on something else?"

"Eh?"

Jase turns to see the record company man and Rhys the Beat, in a ceremonial presentation pose, holding a hard guitar-case. They flip it open to reveal a wine-red, 1960s style Gibson Les Paul Classic. It is the most beautiful inanimate object that Jason Hopkins has ever seen. "What?"

"We were going to give you a guitar anyway – as a thank-you, like".

"What?"

"But with the band breaking up, and you being so helpful this past week, the record company said they could... upgrade it a little."

"I... I don't understand."

Rhys the Bass lays a comforting hand on his shoulder. "It's yours, mate. Courtesy of Cherry Gravy."

"I... I... but... I... but...I... I... but..."

Jase goes on like this for a good few minutes, until the others grow bored, thrust the thing into his hands, and continue with the party.

The others drop Jase off at his mum's on Saturday lunchtime. Dai is waiting there to greet him, and is highly impressed by the Gibson. "Yeah, that'll do, like." They sit in the kitchen, drinking juice, and staring at it. Even Violet, who knows nothing about guitars, feels awed in its presence.

Jase has arranged to get the train down to see Sonia in Cardiff that evening, but is sorely tempted to stay in his bedroom, caressing his gleaming new axe. In the end, however, good sense prevails. And he takes his guitar with him.

CHAPTER NINE

Jase puts about half of his Cherry Gravy money into Ofnadwy Bluesville's kitty, allowing Dai to bring his drum-kit up to scratch, and buying them all matching Ray-Bans, and new crimson shirts. They resume their gigging schedule - mostly pub shows, but also a healthy number of sets at dedicated blues and folk/roots events. As the summer draws to a close, though, and courtesy of the buzz engendered by the RRJ Blues Lamentation experiment, they get invited to play early on the first day of one of the more rock-oriented major festivals in the South of England.

Despite going with their standard short set, which usually serves them well, the crowd remains indifferent – people are still trooping in, and there's a steady, light rain which is dulling the festive mood; not to mention the ink-black clouds creeping down from the North, and the fact that one of the principal headliners pulled out the night before, after collapsing through euphemistic "nervous exhaustion". When "Ain't No Love" fails to get people going, Alun calls Jase over. "There's no point doing 'Fall In Love' – these numbskulls won't appreciate it." Unfortunately, due to a malevolent public address system, this sentiment is relayed to the audience, who are understandably displeased. Amongst the items hurled onto the stage are apple cores, handfuls of mud, and a plastic bottle containing freshly minted urine, which whizzes just past Alun's head. "Sod this for a game of soldiers", he says, and walks off, to the first cheer of the day.

Having anticipated that things might not go entirely smoothly, Jase has allowed himself to be surgically separated from his Gibson, and is reconnecting with his trusty Fender copy. Refusing to panic, he rushes over to Lucy with an idea. She shrugs and relays it to Dai, as Jase wanders to the front of the stage and, for the first time ever at an Ofnadwy Bluesville performance, uses the microphone. "Alright, we'll be off in a bit. Just want to do one more song for you, alright?" Stepping back, he plays the first eight notes of Neil Young's "Like A Hurricane". Without needing a backward glance from their bandleader, Lucy and Dai come in at precisely the same, correct moment, and there follows a lengthy and uncompromising instrumental deconstruction of the piece during which Jase veers wildly between the most basic punkism, and the most impossibly involved Sonny Rollins-esque circuitousness. He ends with a crashing chord which he sustains for a full minute, before raising the guitar above his head and, to the horror of his bandmates, smashing it into the floor. The neck, long since rotting from the inside, snaps on impact. Jase strides off stage, leaving the dying instrument squealing and helpless on the ground. Somewhat less dramatically, Dai and Lucy follow suit.

Backstage, Alun is furious. "What have you done?! Your guitar! I got you that for your thirteenth birthday!"

"You walked off stage. It was unprofessional!"

"They were throwing piss at me, Jason!"

"They were throwing piss at all of us!"

"But... your guitar!"

"It's just another casualty of rock'n'roll, Dad."

Dai sniggers, and Alun does a double-take, but ploughs on. "And what the fuck was that song?"

"Neil Young. He's a genius."

"But... your guitar, Jase!"

Lucy chips in. "That guitar belongs to yesterday."

"Sho' 'nuff", adds Dai, unhelpfully.

When Jase and Dai return to the stage, in their secondary roles as Ofnadwy Bluesville's roadies, they find themselves being cheered by a small section of the crowd, but do not acknowledge them.

After they're all packed up, and Dai and Alun have gone off looking for drugs and "quim" respectively, Lucy and Jase wander together around the park, soaking up the atmosphere, which has improved with the weather. They discuss possible reasons why Jase feels no sting of nostalgic regret at having turned his reliable old guitar into kindling.

"Maybe it's because it pissed your Dad off."

"I don't think so – that's just an added bonus. It just felt like the right thing to do at the time, like. End of an era, kind of thing."

"I guess you're just not one of those blokes who fetishizes consumer durables."

"Only 'cause I could never afford them." He grins. "So, I'm not a fetishist, then. Sonia *will* be disappointed."

They have moved on to consideration of their imminent foreign holiday when they are approached by a trio of local teenage girls.

"It is you, innit?"

"You was on tour with 'Ammerfight!"

Jase nods.

"What are they like?"

Jase smiles, paternal. "They seem like very nice boys."

"My brother says they drink blood, and that."

"They may well do. They seem to drink everything else."

"Are you a lesbian?"

"No, it's just the way I walk."

A titter. "Not you! Her."

"Er... yeah. Is that a problem?"

One of the girls, a mixed-race dyed blonde, indicates her big boned friend. "Her mum's a lesbian."

"Yeah, well, there's a lot of it about."

"You talk funny. Where are you from?", asks the Goth in the Public Enemy tee-shirt.

"Wales."

"Wales? Do you know the Stereophonics?"

"No."

"Do you know the Super Furries?"

"No."

"Do you know the Manics?"

Comedy pause. "No."

"Oh."

"Ooh, look – there's that fit bloke off MTV!"

"See ya!"

And they are gone, skipping like lambs.

"Which one did you fancy?", asks Lucy.

"I'm in love with Sonia. What about you?"

"The fat one was cute." She returns, quickly, to familiar ground. "So, did you really not play around when you were on tour?"

"This again?" He suspects that Sonia has been pestering her for relayed just-between-us-lads banter. "No, no, a thousand times no."

"You must have been tempted."

"Lucy – you're forgetting something. I'm an ugly bloke."

She smiles at him. "Oh yeah. Silly me."

The holiday comes at exactly the right moment for Jase. Still in a daze from the Cherry Gravy experience, he is anxious to break away temporarily, and get some perspective on the Ofnadwy Bluesville project. He has also realised how unpleasant it feels to be away from Sonia for any length of time. With Jase's monetary situation no longer an issue, at least in the short term, she has suggested a romantic weekend away somewhere. Meanwhile, through scouring the Internet, Lucy has spotted a bargain self-catering break in a villa which accommodates four. Already having ascertained that Dai is happy holidaying in his head, and shuddered inwardly at the prospect of Alun rampant on a topless beach, she puts it to Jase that he and Sonia could join her and Carol, who has no compunction about either leaving her child with her mother, or being a financial burden.

They arrive on Corfu ("Not Lesbos?", Alun had joked, inevitably), late on a Sunday night, and even before they have looked over their accommodation, Carol is itching to visit one of the clubs they passed before the coach dropped them off at reception. "But we don't know where we are! How will we find our way back?" Lucy is already wondering how good an idea this trip is.

"You're so boring." But Carol is smiling, and kisses Lucy warmly.

It is a somewhat sterile residence, part of a purpose-built complex, and there is little to choose between the two bedrooms. Instinctively, Jase bagsies the one nearest the bathroom. Disappointment that there is nothing in the fridge soon gives way to recognition of the fact that they are all too tired to do anything about it, and they go straight to bed.

In the morning, Lucy is the first to rise, say "bloody hell" as the heat hits her, and go for a wander. While the sea is plainly visible from the verandah, she discovers that it takes a quarter of an hour to get anywhere near it on foot. Shops are closer, though, and she picks up bread, honey, milk, cheese, and instant coffee.

They spend the first full day as a foursome; hitting the sunbeds in the morning, dozing through the holiday rep's address, lunching on salads and wine, the afternoon siesta back at the villa, a civilised dinner at a traditional taverna. Jase quite enjoys swaggering around in the company of three beautiful women, fancying that he looks a bit like a pimp, but in a good way.

The first split occurs round about midnight, as they queue outside their third club. After three hours of cheesy commercial disco crap pounding in his ears, and English yobbos staring at his woman's peachy bottom in her tight white jeans, Jase has had enough. "Listen girls – I'm getting a headache. I think I'll head back."

"Oh, you boring fucker", complains Carol.

"Shall I come back with you?"

Jase guesses that Sonia's offer does not come from the depths of her being. "Of course not. You stay and enjoy yourself." He belatedly rubs his temples. "I just need a bit of a lie down." He kisses her goodbye, waves at the other two, and strolls off, without a backward glance.

Between the first and second clubs, the party had passed a small bar, whose clientele seemed a little older and more diverse than those of most places they'd noticed. Carol had noted, a tad too loudly, that it looked "boring as shit", and they moved on. Having made a note of its location, though, Jase finds himself there once more. Bouzouki music is playing – not exactly Robert Johnson, but it'll do. Old Greek men in characterful headgear sit around, smoking pipes and playing checkers. There are tourists, too, mostly men. He orders a half-bottle of retsina, and sits in a corner. He gets talking to a Glaswegian bus-driver in his forties, named Henry. He's in the second week of his honeymoon, having married a woman half his age, who is out clubbing with a gang of girls from their hotel. "It's unfair to expect her to want to spend every evening sitting around with an old fart like me."

"But what if she… you know. Other blokes, and that."

Henry smiles, indulgently. "Younger blokes, you mean?" He shrugs. "She's been there, done that."

It is Henry's second marriage. His first ended in divorce after he found her in bed with one of his workmates. "Do you miss him?", jokes Jase. Henry is not amused. Still, he buys him a beer, and they talk about music. Henry is into the crooners – Sinatra, Tony Bennett, Jack Jones, Andy Williams. Jase brings up Scott Walker, but Henry is dismissive of his artiness. They are just bonding over Nat King Cole when Henry's painfully skinny young wife clomps in, her mascara running. She has just escaped the attentions of two youths from Leeds, and tearfully asks to be taken to bed.

"A man's gotta do what a man's gotta do." Henry winks at Jase, as he drains his glass, and walks her out, his hand dwarfing her tiny waist.

Jase does not stay much longer, and as he walks back to the complex, he finds himself wondering what it might be like to be married to Sonia. Strangely, the thought does not scare him, although he concedes that this is probably because the prospect is a distant one, on account of his fiscal instability. When he gets in, he finds himself regretting, for the hundredth time, his decision not to bring his Gibson. It's all part of the perspective thing, though. He pours himself a glass of red wine, reads a little from the hefty book of Raymond Carver short stories that he's brought with him, and gets ready for bed.

He is awoken in the early hours, when Sonia climbs in with him. She is warm and relaxed and giggly. "How's your headache?", she asks.

"All gone", he replies.

"Good", she whispers, slithering down and taking him in her mouth.

If you had told the seventeen-year-old Jason Hopkins that a few years later, he'd spending an entire day on a distant beach, rubbing lotions on and fetching ice-cold drinks for a trio of bare-breasted lovelies, he'd have laughed in your face. After he'd finished playing with himself. The reality, though, begins to grow tiresome after… no, if truth be told, it doesn't grow in the least bit tiresome. Nevertheless, by Tuesday night, the puritan in him is nagging, and over dinner, he suggests to the group that the next day they might do something a little more constructive.

"Oh, don't be so boring", whines Carol. At this point, words cannot express how utterly relieved Jase feels that he never managed to get it together with her. She drags Lucy out clubbing again, and he and Sonia stay in, reading their books and drinking wine before going for a late night walk along the shore-line.

The following day, Jase's counsel having prevailed, they indulge in "activities". Carol and Lucy head out for a tour-company-organised day of beach-oriented frivolity, involving riding around the bay on the back of a large banana, drinking plentiful ridiculously watered-down ouzo, and playing lots of games designed to subvert the concept of personal space.

Jase and Sonia catch a bus to Corfu Town, delightedly taking in the spaghetti western scenery and the impenetrable language of the locals. Once there, they saunter hand in hand through the quaint streets, and wander in and out of shops, Sonia adding to her already extensive collection of tops, and Jase buying novelty bottle-openers inspired by ancient Greek erotica, as souvenirs for Alun and Dai. They lunch in a leisurely manner, stroll around some more, then get the bus back.

They walk in on a bad atmosphere in the villa. The day's activities have included a wet t-shirt contest, in which Carol entered both herself and Lucy as a joke. To the mortification of both of them, Lucy was declared the winner, and Carol is not responding well to her teasing.

"Since when was it a crime to have amazing tits?" Lucy asks Jase and Sonia, rhetorically.

"They've always been your best feature". Jase joins in, cheered by Carol's discomfiture.

Sonia feels ill-equipped to take part in this banter, and busies herself with preparing a bucolic, Hellenic supper of feta cheese, bread, olives and wine.

"So, are you coming out, tonight, Sonia?" Carol's meal-time enquiry sounds more like a demand. "Or are you staying in with this boring tosser again?"

"We thought we'd go somewhere for a quiet drink."

"Quiet drink? We're supposed to be on fucking holiday?"

"This is your idea of a holiday, is it?" Lucy is growing tired of Carol's peevishness. "People doing what you tell them to, rather than deciding for themselves?"

"I'm the only person round here who knows how to have a fucking good time!"

"That would explain the baby, then." Everyone turns to look at Sonia. "Sorry. That was uncalled-for."

Carol shoots her a hooded stare, and finishes her food in silence.

After Carol has dragged Lucy out to clubland, Jase and Sonia make porno love in the bathroom, watching themselves in the mirror, before stepping out to a beachside bar, where they drink bottled lager and stare out at the gently foaming grey sea.

When they get back to the villa, Lucy is there alone and not happy. "Where's Carol?"

Lucy tersely confirms that there has been something of a disagreement. "She went off with some people", she mutters.

Carol is not mentioned again as the three of them polish off a bottle of Apelia Red, and by the time they retire to bed, Lucy seems her cheerful self once more.

Jase is shaken awake at three in the morning. "Wha...?"

"She's just come in! Carol! She's only just come in."

They lie together, listening to the raised voices. Jase realises that he has never heard Lucy shouting in anger before. It is slightly scary. They cannot make out many words until one sentence rings out, shrill and clear in the night. "I just fancied a bit of dick, that's all!"

Sonia gasps, and claps a hand over her mouth. "Shit! What's she done?"

Presently, they hear the bedroom door slam, and all is silence. Jase gets up to go to the toilet. It is not till he is on the way back that he notices Lucy, sitting alone in the moonlit kitchen. He wanders over to her. "Hiya, Luce. Er, Carol not back yet?"

Lucy smiles sadly. "You'll never get an Oscar, Jase. She's been out having a good time." Her prize for winning the contest was a large bottle of the local brandy, from which she is now pouring herself a second generous glassful. "She's been out being a good time."

"Oh." Jase rests a hand on her shoulder. "Will you be alright?"

"Don't know." She sighs. "You couldn't do me a favour, could you?"

Jase returns to his and Sonia's bedroom. "What's happening?", stage-whispers Sonia. Jase puts a finger to his lips, goes to the wardrobe, and takes out the spare pillow and blanket. He returns to the kitchen, having first placed the bedding on the sofa.

"Do you think this is a good idea?"

"I just can't be with her right now." She is crying, which causes a wrenching feeling in Jase's chest.

"She doesn't deserve you." He kisses her forehead, and goes back to Sonia.

"Well?"

Jase shakes his head. "It doesn't look good."

He gets back into bed, and they hold one another, trying not to feel complacent.

Jase rises early, and peers out into the living area. Carol is clattering around the kitchen. Lucy appears to be fast asleep on the sofa. "Morning," he says.

"What the fuck's it got to do with you?", squawks Carol.

Jase rolls his eyes, and goes to the bathroom. By the time he emerges, Carol has disappeared back into the girls' bedroom. Jase approaches Lucy. She is snoring gently, and her face is marked with the tracks of her tears. "Poor baby."

On his return to their bedroom, Sonia is awake. "Well?"

"It doesn't look good."

"Shit. What are we going to do?"

Jase shrugs. "Keep out of it. Fancy an early morning stroll?"

"Aren't you going to do anything? They're your friends!"

"Lucy's my friend. Carol's my other friend's sister." He starts changing into his going-out shorts. "And a pain in the arse."

Sonia watches him dress, in astonishment. "What are you doing."

"I've spent enough of my life getting caught in the fucking crossfire. I shall be breakfasting in the open air." He sits on the bed, and kisses her. "Coming?"

Sonia sighs a weight-of-the-world sigh. "Maybe I should try and... do something."

"Yes – try and butt out. This is not your problem."

"It is if they fuck up our holiday!"

"We don't have to let them." He gently caresses her shoulder. "Let's just leave them to deal with their own shit, okay?"

Sonia settles back under the bedsheet. "You go for your walk, love. I'll have a lie-in."

"Sonia!" Jase attempts a stern tone. "You are not getting involved in this!"

Sonia smiles, defiant. "Are you attempting to give me an order, Jason Hopkins?"

"It's not an order. It's a... suggestion."

"Didn't sound like a suggestion."

"Alright!" Jase throws up his hands in despair. "You do what you want. I'm going out."

Jase wanders down to the beach, takes a seat at a ramshackle eatery, and orders some baklava and a black coffee. The youngish but near-toothless proprietor smiles at him. "Ah – the man with the three women!"

Jase chuckles. "It's not as much fun as it looks." He explains the situation, omitting the lesbian element, just in case.

"Ah. You make wise decision, my friend. When women fight..." he makes the universal hand gesture for "get the hell out of there."

They chat for a while, until the subject veers dangerously close to "So, what are black women like in bed?" territory. By this time, however, Jase has been joined by other customers, and he is able take his leave discreetly. He strolls on up the shoreline, and sits on some rocks, watching a gang of insouciant fishermen, direct from Central Casting, toying meaningfully with their nets. Despite having avoided shellfish for many years, he has a sudden craving for a prawn mayonnaise sandwich.

Returning to the villa, he pauses outside and listens at the door for sounds of combat. Hearing nothing, he pops his head in. He sees only Lucy, eating breakfast.

"Hiya, Luce. Sonia not up yet?"

"She's been up. And now she's hiding." Lucy sighs, and shakes her head. "You should have warned her about not getting involved." She gulps. "I think I called her an interfering cow."

"Oh. Have you apologised."

"I'm sure I'll get round to it."

"Right. And what about Carol?"

"That slut? Who gives a fuck?"

Jase is not tempted to investigate further. He knocks before re-entering his and Sonia's bedroom. She is curled up underneath the sheet, with her back to him. "Babe? Lucy says she's sorry," he lies.

She sniffles. "Why don't you say what you're dying to say?"

"I told you so."

"Bastard."

He peels off his clothes and gets under the sheet with her. "I'm not in the mood", she says, as he makes spoons with her.

"Neither am I. Big breakfast." He smiles to himself. "Hey – did I ever tell you my Mam was dyslexic?"

"What?"

"Yeah. Every winter she used to send me to school with a baklava on my head."

Sonia laughs despite herself, and they fall into a light, almost-contented sleep.

When they emerge once more into the body of the villa, the atmosphere, despite an ambient temperature well into the 80s, is icy. Lucy is sitting on the sofa, reading her book – she has borrowed Jase's Brando autobiography. Carol is ostentatiously applying her make-up in the kitchen. Seeing the happier couple appear, she mooches in. "I want to get the bus into Corfu town. See what the shopping's like. Come with me, one of you?"

Jase and Sonia look at one another, and draw telepathic straws. Sonia loses. "Sure. I'll just get my shit together."

They are gone within the half-hour – but not before Lucy has taken Sonia aside to apologise for referring to her as livestock.

With Carol out of the house, the mood lightens somewhat. Jase sits next to Lucy, and rests a hand on her knee. "Listen, Luce – I'm sorry. I mean, if we'd gone out with you last night, maybe she wouldn't have... wouldn't have..."

"Had a threesome with a couple of hairy-arsed firemen from Colwyn Bay?"

"Shit!" Jase cannot keep an image from coming to mind. "When... when you say 'threesome'..."

Lucy shoots a Star Wars-style laser-beam from her eyes, just missing his head. "I haven't asked her."

"No, it's just, she's had two at the same time before. Dai told me."

"Why are we having this conversation?"

"Brothers they were. Imagine that! Rubbing up against your own brother's stiffie!"

"Will you shut up?"

"Might be alright at the time, like, but you'd get a complex afterwards."

"Are you still talking?"

"I mean, does that count as gay?"

"Shut the fuck up!"

"I suppose, technically, it's incest."

"Jason – has anyone ever told you you're an insensitive, ignorant little prick!"

"Oh, yeah. Happens all the time."

She glares at him. He smiles apologetically. Without knowing why, she giggles. Then, her face crumples, and she starts to cry. She grabs hold of him, burying her face in his chest, whimpering and snivelling fit to break his heart in two. By the time she has finished, his t-shirt is ruined. It's not the tears he minds – it's the snot. Just as well it was a plain one, not his cherished Marilyn Monroe, that Sonia got him for his birthday. When she is cried out, she goes to the bathroom to dry her eyes. Jase reflects smugly on having done his good deed for the day.

They decide to risk lunching in one of the gaudy restaurants along the main tourist drag. While Lucy has the moussaka, Jase plumps for the Ocean Platter. Lucy jokes that she should be the one with a taste for seafood, and Jase admonishes her for resorting to off-colour, homophobic humour.

"Mind you, though – I could never afford a meal like this back home. Octopus? Lobster? Oysters? Whatever this little thing is? Shit, is it still moving?" He stabs it, and shoves it into his mouth, chowing down merrily. "Strange, isn't it – sometimes, for no reason at all, you fancy something you haven't had for ages."

"Well, I suppose I should be grateful that you're at least progressed to double entendres", says Lucy, pouring herself a third glass of wine.

Jase gulps. "I… I didn't mean… I wasn't talking about… erm…" He shuts up, and concentrates on his food.

A very few minutes into a post-prandial walk, Jase recalls with a rumbling dismay the reason why he has for so long forsaken the fruits of the sea. "Erm… got to get back." He breaks into an unaccustomed sprint, and it is only superhuman willpower, combined with the British horror of public embarrassment, which enables him to maintain sphincter control until he reaches the bathroom of the villa, whereupon he sits, with a sigh, on the lavatory, and allows everything he's ingested for the past six weeks to extravagantly vacate his body, in liquid form.

When Lucy comes in, a few minutes later, he is lying, exhausted, on the sofa. She grins at him. "Projectile defecation?"

"No, thanks, I've just had one. But that's a great name for a band!"

On the way back, she has bought diarrhoea tablets and a large bottle of water. "Here's your medication." She's also purchased a litre of wine. "And this is mine."

They sit there for a while, listening to his intestines making diverting noises, maintaining their fluid intake, and talking about relationships.

"Well, there goes my theory about the whole lesbian thing being cool, because women don't mess one another around," says Jase.

"You really don't get out much, do you?"

"Mind you… it pales in comparison with…" He tells her some of Alun's stories about Dai's uncle Marto, and his many unsuitable boyfriends.

"Yeah. Men are bastards. Women are bastards. What ya gonna do?"

"Uh-oh" Jase feels moved to roll hurriedly off the sofa, and once more into the bathroom, this time marginally less productively. By the time he feels secure enough to return, Lucy has finished the wine, and is tackling the remnants of her brandy. "What were you doing in there? Off-loading some vital organs?"

"Felt like it. I think I'll crash out."

Once in the bedroom, Jase closes the shades, and goes foetal on top of the bedsheet. He falls asleep almost immediately, only awakening briefly a half-hour or so later, when Lucy opens the door. "Sorry. Don't feel like being alone." She clambers onto the bed, behind him, resting a hand on his fore-arm. Both lose consciousness once more.

When Jase next wakes up, he is lying on his back. He looks down. He has an erection. Lucy's sleepy head is on his shoulder. Saliva trickles from the corner of her mouth. "Lucy?"

"Hm?", she murmurs. Her hand drifts dreamily to his middle. Suddenly they are both wide awake.

"Sorry", says Jase. "Reflex."

Lucy freezes. Then, she starts to gently stroke the bulge. It responds.

"I think you'd better stop doing that", says Jase.

Lucy's fingers stray to the waistband of his shorts. She tugs it down, allowing the tumescent organ to spring free. She looks at it. "Cool", she whispers.

"You're drunk."

Lucy takes a deep breath, then leaps off the bed. Quickly she pulls down her pants, and steps out of them. She leaps back onto the bed, kneeling beside him. The erect penis grows more attentive. "Tell me no."

"What?"

"Say 'no'".

Jase opens his mouth to speak. But the word which emerges is "God".

Lucy straddles him, eases him inside her with firm fingers, and begins to gently undulate, eyes closed, biting her bottom lip. Jase has little difficulty in ensuring that his mind is elsewhere, since he is struggling to monitor the low-level grumbling in his innards, desperate for an accident of epic grossness not to occur. He wonders where to look – the look of dazed concentration on Lucy's soft face excites him; closing his eyes makes him imagine that he is with Sonia, which is even more stimulating. He turns his head, fixing his gaze on the plastic-carrier-bag in which he is stashing his dirty laundry. By the time Lucy's gasps and motions indicate that she is reaching a crucial moment, he can resist no longer. Turning back to face her, he reaches forward, and pulls up her t-shirt, watching the prize-winning breasts quiver sumptuously as she writhes above him. He climaxes first, crying out, and she follows in short order, collapsing onto him, with what sounds like a sob.

They lie together, wordless, for several minutes, until something starts to rise in Jase's stomach. "Shit!" He hastily disengages from her, and dashes to the bathroom, where he vomits loudly and copiously into the toilet-bowl. As he washes his face, he looks at himself in the mirror. "Shit!"

He wraps a towel around his waist, and walks out into the lounge area. Lucy, dressed once more, is sitting on the sofa, head in hands. "This is the effect I have on men. Now you know why I became a lesbian."

"I'm sorry", says Jase.

"You didn't do anything", Lucy replies. "Well, you did, but… you know. Under duress."

"I wouldn't put it quite like that."

"Listen… I was… I'm sorry. I was being selfish. Treating you like a… you know. Like some sort of… toy. "

"Oh." Jase gives a hollow chuckle. "For future reference, blokes don't really mind that kind of thing, on the whole."

"Right. Duly noted."

"Listen… Lucy… you know I've always been a little in love with you."

"Of course. You're only human." The giggle which follows carries more than a hint of hysteria. "Sorry. Still drunk."

"But… I'm a lot in love with Sonia."

"I know. I understand. This won't happen again. It didn't even happen this time."

"Great. Thanks." He starts to make for the bedroom, then pauses. "Erm… can I… can I ask a question?"

"Yes, darling, you were wonderful."

"I'm serious."

Lucy reaches out a hand. Jase takes it. "It was very nice, Jason. Really. But you haven't miraculously cured me of the gayness."

"Oh. Good."

CHAPTER TEN

Jase actually begins to think that they can get away with it.

When Sonia and Carol come in that evening, he and Lucy are seated side by side on the sofa, reading their books, "like a couple of old women", according to Carol. Jase explains the medical ramifications of the Ocean Platter, and Sonia insists that she'll have to break the date she made with Carol while shopping, and stay in with him. They enjoy a cosy evening together, while Carol coaxes Lucy to "come out for a quiet drink – I mean it – and a serious chat about things." He convincingly pretends to share Sonia's innocent awe, as they listen together in bed to Carol and Lucy making love very loudly, after they come in late and laughing. They spend much of the next day as a sunbathing foursome once more, and Jase is painfully scrupulous as regards making as much eye-contact with Lucy as before, and not avoiding idle, jokey conversation or close physical proximity. The occasional knowing glance is shared, just sufficient for mutual reassurance that what happened had some as-yet undetermined meaning, some emotional impact. In the evening, they split into couples once more, Jase and Sonia going for an up-market meal, devoid of fish, and Lucy and Carol opting for kebabs and dancing. The following day, they have to be packed and out of the villa by midday, and even though the bus which will take them back to the airport isn't due to arrive until late that evening, and tempers fray as they lug their bags from bar to beach to café, no-one cracks.

Jefferson, Violet's boyfriend, attempting to curry favour with Jase, has agreed to pick them up from Bristol Airport. Having spent much of his life as an observer, he notices something of an atmosphere in the back of his cab, even as Carol, in the front with him, cheerily imparts selected details of her good time. The mood appears to lighten after he drops Sonia off in Cardiff, although the warmth with which she and Jase kiss goodbye appears to suggest that there is certainly nothing wrong there. The bulk of his attention, however, is taken up with contemplation of Jase's skin. While it would be going far too far to suggest that the boy now has a tan, his customary pallor has given way to a gentle rosiness. "I see you caught the sun, then, Jason."

"Bit hard to avoid it, like, Jeff."

The way it all goes bad is as follows: at some point in the next few days, Carol and Lucy find themselves able to joke about Carol's threesome, as its significance rapidly decreases in consequentiality. Carol decrees that Lucy now has the freedom to have an affair of her own, but only with a man, so that it won't count. Lucy quips that maybe she already has. Carol detects some steel beneath the joviality, and begins to dig deeper. After all, they've hardly been apart since it's happened, and the only even tangentially male person Lucy has been close to within the past few days is… "Jase!"

"Oh… of course not, don't be stupid."

"Look into my eyes!"

"Piss off!"

"I mean it – look at me!"

"Leave me alone!"

Et cetera, et cetera, ad nauseam, until Lucy disintegrates, tearfully.

Jase comes to convince himself that he might well have confessed to Sonia had they been able to see each other in the week following the holiday. The Tuesday after she jets back, though, is the start of a three-day team-building exercise in the Brecon Beacons with the rest of her work-mates, and they won't be able to get together again until the weekend. By which time she has received the call, on her mobile, from a scandalised Carol.

"Jase? Is it true?" There is more fear than anger in Sonia's voice. It is late on Thursday evening, and she is sitting, trembling, on her bed, having just got home.

"Is what true?"

"Don't be obtuse. You know what."

Jase does, having been warned by Dai. "I... I don't know what you want me to say."

"How long has it been going on?"

"How long has what been going on?"

"You and Lucy."

"It hasn't. I mean... it was only once. It was... an accident."

"An accident? You accidentally stuck your dick in her?!"

Jase cringes, as he freezes in his mother's hallway. He has barely slept all week. "I mean... it was a mistake. It wasn't supposed to happen. I'm sorry."

"You're sorry? You're sorry?!"

"Yes. I wish it hadn't happened. But it has. It did. And I'm sorry."

"Well, it's not fucking good enough, is it?"

"I know."

"I don't like being laughed at, Jason."

"What?"

"You and her. Laughing at me."

"It's not like that."

"She's my friend! I thought she was my friend."

"She's not laughing at you. It was just... it wasn't supposed to happen. She didn't mean to... she was drunk."

"Oh, so you're telling me she raped you, is that it?"

"No. It... it wasn't like that."

"What *was* it like?"

"I'm not going to answer that."

"I trusted you. I thought you were different."

"I know. I'm sorry."

"I thought you loved me."

"I do. I do love you. More than... more than..."

"I know how you've always felt about her."

"She's... I love her like a sister. I mean... like a friend. But the way I love you... that's... you're the best thing that's ever happened to me. And I've hurt you, and I'm sorry. I'm sorry."

"I trusted you."

"I know."

"I thought we had something special. Something real."

On this last word, her voice cracks, and Jase feels his heart snap clean in two. "I... I love you, Sonia. I'm sorry. I don't know what else I can say. I don't know what you want me to say." He pauses, his throat closing up. "No, I... I do know. You want me to beg you to forgive me. I'm not going to do that. I don't deserve to be forgiven. I did something wrong, and that's that. I don't deserve to be forgiven. I don't deserve you."

Sonia is unable to speak for a while. Finally: "You bastard."

She hangs up.

Jase has not cried since he was going cold turkey. He doesn't cry now, except that when he finally goes to sleep, on Friday night, he has a dream in which his mother has left him alone in the supermarket just as it's closing, and when he wakes up he hears himself bawling like a baby, and has to get up and fetch a towel to wipe his face. But that doesn't really count. Mostly he feels numb. Numb and dumb.

The next band practice is on Sunday morning. Lucy arrives early. Self-consciously, she keeps her distance. "I'm so sorry, Jase."

"Yeah. Whatever. Shit happens."

"I called her. I phoned. She wouldn't talk to me. She kept hanging up. I think she pulled the plug out, in the end."

"It's not your problem, Luce."

"I feel terrible."

"So, how are things with Carol?"

"Oh. You know. We're getting there."

"Glad to hear it."

"I'm so sorry, Jase."

"Yeah. Well."

When Alun turns up, he jokingly pretends to warm his hands on Jase's new pink face. He is unsurprised when this does not raise a laugh. What does surprise him, though, is how often Dai and Jase appear to be hugging one another. In contrast, Lucy lingers on the outskirts, saying little.

"Erm... look... am I missing something?"

Dai look to Jase for permission before explaining. "Jase and Sonia... they've split up, like."

"Oh. Oh, shit, Jase." He goes to his son and embraces him. "Oh, Jase. She's... she was... you were so good together, mun."

"Yeah."

"What happened?"

"Oh, you know." A flickered glance at Lucy, who is intently micro-tuning her bass. "Holiday shit."

"Yeah – they can be a killer, holidays."

Alun's travel experiences, on the other hand, have been entirely positive. Fulfilling a lifetime's ambition, he has paid his first-ever visit to Amsterdam. During the week-long break, he took in all the sites of special scientific interest – the Sex Museum, the Red Light Area, the Banana Bar – as well as stocking up on hard-core pornography. He also worked his way through a middle-aged hen-party from Dublin, although not the bride-to-be, since that would have been unethical; added to the fact that she was the ugly one. He ran into one of them again on his last day, in the queue to get into the Anne Frank House. Her name was Miriam, and like him, she figured that she might as well do something vaguely constructive to make up for the hedonism. Afterwards, duly chastened, they had a quiet cup of "special" tea in a café, and chatted about life, before going back to his hotel room.

"I mean, I know I'm supposed to be a dirty old man, and all that. But the older I get… young girls, like… I'm starting to find them fucking irritating."

"Really, Dad?"

"You know what they say – old fiddle, good tune."

"Yeah. Okay, Dad."

"That's what you should do. Go for an older woman, next time. So you get gratitude combined with experience. That'll put some hairs on your chest."

"Erm… can we get on?"

They run through their full set, aiming to iron out any rustiness, and look over their list of engagements for the next couple of months, which is highly encouraging.

"Ofnadwy Bluesville are back in full effect, eh son?"

"Yeah, Dad. Great."

"Dear Sonia,

This is a very hard letter for me to write, but, frankly, that's my problem. I just want to say what I need to say and not waste too much of your time.

What happened with Jase in Corfu was a mistake. I was drunk, and he was in a weakened state, but that's no excuse. I was upset about Carol, and I wasn't thinking about anybody's feelings except mine. It wasn't seduction, or making love, or anything like that. It was just a physical thing. We didn't even kiss.

Reading that bit back it looks horrible and cold-blooded. It wasn't like that. It was just a drunken, stupid mistake, and I'm sorry.

I know you're feeling hurt right now, and I understand that. I would feel exactly the same way. All I know, though, is that Jase loves you very much indeed, and he's hurting like crazy. And I know you love him. And you're both my friends, and I hope you can sort this out, because it's a lonely world, and when you have something special, you shouldn't let a fuck-wit like me spoil it for you.

Jase didn't ask me to write this. Deep down, this is probably just me being selfish again, trying to make myself feel less bad.

I'll stop now because I'm getting suicidal. Which I know you probably wouldn't have a problem with.

I'm sorry.

Love,

Lucy T."

Over the next few weeks, Jase spends a lot of time in his room, playing his Gibson, losing himself in his music. It actually seems to ease the pain, at least momentarily.

He continues to work for the Khans. They only met Sonia once, when she came up to visit, and went out on a couple of deliveries with him, then got bored, and stayed in the shop with them, chatting and eating samosas. "It's a pity", says Samira. "She was lovely." Jase has no option but to agree.

On a trip to the shops for his mum one afternoon, Jase realises that he is being shadowed. He turns, and sees Teg and Bumpy walking several paces behind him.

"What do you bastards want?"

"Whoa, whoa." Teg makes a placatory gesture. "You're a mate. We haven't spoken in ages."

"I've been busy."

"Your band's doing quite well. For what it is, like."

"Heard about your girlfriend dumping you." Bumpy nods, gravely. "They're all bitches, innit?"

"Shut the fuck up, Bumpy." Teg smiles at Jase. "You're in pain, mate, I can see that. You've had a lot of pain in your life. We've known each other a long time. I remember the days. Eh, Jase? The days when you used to come to me for something so life wouldn't hurt so much? Well, guess what, Jase…" He opens his arms, the picture of magnanimity. "I'm still here."

With a low, animal growl, Jase launches himself head-first at Teg, getting in a couple of good punches to the face before Bumpy realises what is going on, and drags him off, slamming him into the wall of the butcher's. "Oi!"

Teg takes a number of deep breaths. "Alright. Alright, Jase. I'll let you have that one for free." He feels his nose, anxious about permanent damage. "But the next time you come to me – and believe me, you will, because once a fucking junkie, always a fucking junkie – the next time you come to me, there will be no preferential rates. Capisce?"

He turns and walks away. Before joining, Bumpy delivers a mighty slap to the side of Jase's head. "We never warn anyone twice, Hopkins."

A month or so later, Jase is still finding little difficulty in resisting Teg's open invitation. He supposes that a part of him is applauding his resolve, in a self-satisfied manner, but it's not at the forefront of his mind.

What is is the fact that there has been no contact with Sonia, other than a small package which arrived in the week following their last phone conversation. It included two CDs which he'd lent her (Nino Rota film music, and some Jimmy Smith Hammond organ jazz), his toothbrush, and a pair of his underpants which she'd put in with her washing a few weeks earlier and forgotten to separate out. Nothing else, not even a note.

The Ofnadwy Bluesville adventure continues to provide a lifeline. The latest highlight is their most high-profile London gig to date. They've played pubs on the outskirts before, testing the water. But this is as a result of a direct invitation from a dedicated venue, in the capital's buzzing West End. It's a Saturday night, too, so a healthy crowd is assured.

It has not escaped Alun's attention that his son has been in a waking coma ever since the split with Sonia. He chooses not to intervene, knowing full well that this would not be welcomed. And, in any case, it doesn't seem to have affected the band. If anything, Jase's playing has improved. "I guess that's why they call it the blues", he jokes, making sure that no-one hears him. Lucy appears to be traumatised as well, although that's understandable, since she was there, on holiday with them, and probably watched the whole thing fall apart. They seem less pally, as well, Jase and Lucy, which is a pity. More than once, though, during moments of solitary pleasure, Alun has given found himself speculating over whether Jase caught Lucy and Sonia in bed together. But he feels it would be rude to ask.

The London gig goes smoothly, although "Misunderstood", the grand finale, seems to fall a little flat, possibly because Lucy fails to reciprocate when Jase looks over at her, and their duelling solos appear to inhabit separate universes. The audience doesn't seem to mind, though, and the offers of post-show drinks are both numerous and gratefully received.

"Jase?"

The voice is familiar. Nursing his beer in what passes for a quiet corner in these parts, Jase looks up. "Bloody hell! Gavin!"

It is the former lead singer of Cherry Gravy. "You were really good. Really good."

"Don't sound so surprised, mate."

"Sorry. It's just… I mean, I've never seen you before. Not with these. I know you've got a good reputation back home, but…well, my hopes weren't high."

"Fair enough."

"Erm… join us?"

With nothing better to do, Jase follows Gavin to his table, at which sit his wife, Amy, whom Jase knows by sight, and a man in his thirties, in whose eyes he discerns the fiery stoicism of yet another former junkie. "Hiya, Jason. I'm Hugo."

It transpires that Hugo was the executive who signed Cherry Gravy to their major record deal. As is the way of things, though, he departed the company shortly afterwards, which explains, to a degree, the lack of support given to their second album. Added, of course, to the already-established fact that it was shite.

"So, you two are still friends, then?"

"Not just friends. Colleagues."

Since leaving the record-company, Hugo has set up an independent label of his own. Gavin has recently joined him as a partner and creative director, having moved to London with Amy, whose family is from there, anyway. "I mean, the singles market's fucked, we know this. But there are still ways of making money out of it." Jase has never seen Gavin so animated. "And having a good time. The cottage industry approach, that's the future. And the Internet, obviously. But people like singles. They like them as objects. What they don't like is being ripped off."

Jase is pleasantly stunned to learn that in the few months since the Cherry Gravy debacle, Gavin has been involved in two top 20 hit singles. The first, which he produced, was by an indie guitar band from North Wales, who've since had their contract lucratively (for Hugo and Jase, at any rate) bought out by a major. The second was one of those dance hits which sampled elements from two songs from the 1980s, put together by Gavin and his old bandmate DJ Dwm. "Yes, we know it was crap." Hugo responds to Jase's instinctive sneer. "But it sold absolute tonnes in Europe. We made money, the original artists made money, some E'd-up kids had a passable record to dance to – everybody's happy."

"Listen, Jase… we've been talking." Gavin smiles, fiendishly. "How would you like to have a hit record?"

Since the rest of Ofnadwy Bluesville have been expecting to drive back to Wales overnight, it is not hard to round them up. Jase joins Hugo, Gavin and Amy in Hugo's Range Rover, and the others follow them in the minibus, driven by Lucy. As they disembark outside Hugo's impressive residence in Bayswater, Alun whistles his approval. "How the other half live, eh?"

Hugo smiles. "Well, it's amazing what you can afford in London if you have contacts. And a half-decent job. And if you manage to resist spending all your money on cocaine."

A few minutes later, after Hugo and Gavin explain the plan, Alun's eyes are sparkling. "Well, I've heard worse ideas in my life."

Left alone for a few minutes, Ofnadwy Bluesville discuss their options, both creatively and business-wise. In very short order, Hugo and Gavin are called back into the room. Understandably, given the nature of his operation, Hugo has plentiful copies of his standard contract to hand, and they all sign them. With a busy day ahead, and the time approaching 3 a.m., both Gavin and Hugo make offers of accommodation.

"Dai and me'll come with you, Gav, if that's okay." Jase guesses correctly that leaving a current junkie in the care of a former junkie would be a recipe for conflict. It also means that Jase doesn't have to spend time alone with either Lucy or his father, which is also good. Although he seems to notice a some regret in Lucy's expression as he takes his leave. But maybe that's because, these days, shamefully, he quite enjoys it when she appears to be unhappy.

Back at Gavin and Amy's relatively modest two-bedroom flat in East Dulwich, Jase and Dai enjoy a swift whisky with them before retiring. Jase is only mildly alarmed at having to share a bed with his oldest friend.

"I don't have a very good record when it comes to sleeping with my mates."

"Erm... I think that's in bad taste, Jase." Dai is uncharacteristically sombre.

"You okay?" Jase has not kept a track of whether or not Dai has had time to see to his habit.

"It's this record thing. I just get the feeling we're going to be ripped off."

"It's the music business, Dai. Of course we're going to get ripped off. It's all part of the fun."

Back at Hugo's, meanwhile, Lucy and Alun sit sleeplessly watching vintage rock videos on their host's massive plasma-screen TV, having been told to make themselves at home. She is just taking a deep breath prior to confessing all about her accidental fling with his son, when he finally takes the opportunity to ask an intimate question about the nature of her bedtime arrangements with Carol. She makes her excuses and takes her leave.

Both parties arrive at the studio well before the appointed hour of midday; although Gavin is alarmed when Dai goes walkies in the early morning. Jase reassures him, though, that despite his "personal health issues", Dai has never let his band-mates down and, true to form, he turns up five minutes before the off, looking as perky as he ever does. "Hey, dudes, come on, let's go make some hits!"

Lucy is the only member of Ofnadwy Bluesville who has never before experienced a professional recording set-up, and she is well-practised when it comes to taking things in her stride, so the awe is kept to a minimum. In any case, she seizes the opportunity to have a nose around while Dai is acquainting himself with the drum-kit in the studio's live room, which he's been asked to use in order to save valuable setting-up time. She is impressed.

"Okay, guys – when you're ready."

Ofnadwy Bluesville perform their handshake ritual, then, with the tape rolling, run through their seven-song "short" set, without a break and without Alun's patter. Listening through to it afterwards, all present agree that "Yer Blues" is ropey (and there's no way they're putting out a Beatles song as a debut single, in any case), and that "Misunderstood" has failed to translate well to the studio context. Gavin argues that the bass on "Old Man Trouble" is too upfront for it to work well on the radio, and Hugo suggests that "Grapevine" is too obvious a choice. Which leaves "Touch The Hem Of His Garment", which is unrepresentative of the band's general ethos; "Ain't No Love In The Heart Of The City", their treatment of which is perhaps a little too raw to make it a commercial proposition; and "It Looks Like I'm Never Gonna Fall In Love Again."

They put it to the vote, and the result is three to one, Jase being the dissenting voice. "I don't know, it just sounds a bit... cheesy."

Gavin sighs. "Frankly, Jase, cheese is the market we're going for."

"Blue cheese!", quips Dai.

"That's all well and good, but... but..."

"So it's back to square one, is it?" Alun is annoyed. "Your band, your rules?"

"No, no, of course not, but..."

"This isn't just about you, Jason." Lucy sounds unusually harsh. "This is our chance to... get somewhere. Make some money."

"I know, I know, it's just..." Jase trails off.

"Erm... there is another issue." Hugo explains that if they want to maximise their earnings, a good idea might be to couple whatever cover version they choose with a song of their own. "A B-side, as it were."

"But we don't do song-writing", protests Alun. "We're interpretationists!"

Dai is already making his way to the drum-kit. "Come on, kids. Time's a-wastin'!" He starts up a punky, propulsive beat. Jase leaps to his feet and runs over, and they commence one of their uncompromising hard-core jams. Alun and Lucy exchange a "for fuck's sake!" look, as they amble over. Lucy pointedly refuses to take part in the mayhem, and Alun ostentatiously indicates his watch.

"May I remind you that we're guests?"

Jase smiles mischievously, for the first time in several weeks. "Sorry. Dai?"

The drummer nods, and segues seamlessly into something a little less frenzied, but still a bit heavy metal for their purposes, as Lucy demonstrates by playing Deep Purple's "Smoke On The Water" over it.

"Try something jazzy", shouts Alun. Dai responds by playing several bars in 7/4 time, which just confuses everybody.

"Sorry", he says. "Too clever for my own good, me." He then starts off a shuffle rhythm, of the kind which might have accompanied a striptease artist in more sedate times.

Alun smiles, and nods. "Yeah. Yeah, that's good." He closes his eyes, feeling the vibe, so to speak. "Slow it down a bit, Dai, mate."

Dai complies, and Lucy joins in, with a fairly basic progression, reminiscent of something from the swing era. After a few bars, Jase contributes a trad bluesy riff, which seems to fit, and he repeats it. A few minutes in, they seem to have found a comfortable space in which to work. "Okay", croons Alun. "Ain't nobody's business – ain't nobody's business."

The others look at one another, slightly puzzled. Alun's eyes are still closed, as though he is channelling messages from the other side.

"They say I play around with the ladies", he begins, coming across as though Rex Harrison in "My Fair Lady", were being understudied by a cheeky chappie former miner from the South Wales Valleys. "And the ladies play around with me... but that's okay – ain't nobody's damn business but mine. Yeah!"

The riffing continues. Lucy looks over at Jase, and smiles tentatively. He twitches the corners of his mouth, half-encouragingly. This turns into a proper smile as Alun points in Lucy's direction.

"They say I act inappropriate for my gender... yeah... they make all kinds of insinuations... but that's okay – ain't nobody's damn business but mine."

Lucy glares at the back of Alun's head. This makes Jase laugh, and the riff mutates into a brief, snappy solo, before returning home. Alun then points at Dai.

"They say my eyes go round and round in my head... they say I'm gonna wind up dead... but what the hell - ain't nobody's damn business but mine."

Lucy is open-mouthed in horror, but Dai remains impassive, never varying his beat for an instant. They plough along in the groove for a while, Jase slipping in a fancy lick here and there, before Alun points to him. Jase gulps.

"They tell me I'm a loser... ain't never gonna amount to nothing... but I say... the only thing that's anybody's damn business... is the way I play this old guitar of mine... play the guitar, son!"

He punches the air, as a cue for Jase to go into an extended, playful, facetious solo, direct from the 1950s, calling on the spirits of Jimmy Reed, Elmore James, John Lee Hooker; concluding with an incisive minor 9th which verges on the discordant.

"Yeah... they say we're fools... doing what we do... but do we care? The hell we do! Well, alright... nobody's damn business... nobody's business..."

Alun steps away from the mic, head down, and the band chug along for another minute or so, until they get the nod from Hugo and Gavin, whereupon the song fizzles out anti-climactically.

"Bloody hell, Dad, where did that come from?"

"I'm a poet of the streets, mun! Did I never tell you?"

Jase is washing his hands after a visit to the toilet, when he hears the door swing open and shut behind him. He smiles. "Not bad going, eh." He turns and is shocked to see Lucy standing there, arms wide, blocking his exit.

"We need to talk."

"Erm... we've got to get back, Luce. We haven't got long."

"There are things we've got to talk about."

"We can talk on the drive home."

"Alone. We need to talk alone."

"You shouldn't even be in here, Lucy."

"I'm late. My period. It's late."

A cartoon anvil falls on Jase's head, causing him to see double. His knees start to buckle. "W-what?"

"I've missed a period. I'm pregnant."

"Erm… I… well… how… erm… is it… is it…"

"Is it yours? Of course it's fucking yours!"

"But… but… how?"

"That's not the most intelligent thing you've ever said, Jase."

"Couldn't… are you sure?"

"Pretty sure."

"Oh." A million questions buzz around inside his head. How to pick out the one which won't make him feel even more of an idiot? "What about Carol?"

"Carol is unable to produce sperm, Jase."

"That's not what I… does she know?"

"Yes." Lucy sighs. "She knows, alright."

"Oh. What did she say?"

"Leaving out the swearing? Not a great deal."

"Oh." Jase forces a shaky half-smile. "What do you want to do?"

"I… I… I don't know." Her bottom lips starts to quiver, and all of a sudden she looks like a frightened little girl. "What do you think I should do?"

This shocks him. "Me? Does it matter what I think?"

"It's your child, Jason."

"Yes. Yes." He looks away, songs from other planets playing in his ears. "I just assumed I'd never… you know… that no-one would ever…." He shakes his head, and clears his throat. "Do you want to have the baby?"

"I don't know, Jase. I'm... things are... difficult. Things are... uncertain."

"Do you want to get married."

She jumps. "You what?"

"We'll have it. We'll get married."

"I'm not marrying you, Jason. I love Carol. And you love... I'm with Carol."

"Have the baby. I mean...if it was up to me, if it was any of my business... I mean, I don't want to meddle, and it's got to be entirely your decision, and if you don't want it, that's fine. But I think you should have it."

"Do you?" Lucy frowns. "But... I'm a kid myself."

"You're pushing thirty, Luce. And you're the most sensible person, like, ever. You can do this. We can do this."

"We?"

"You and me and Carol."

"Okay, now that just sounds fucking weird."

"This whole conversation's a bit strange, let's face it." He walks over to her, just managing to keep his balance. He puts his hands on her shoulders and looks into her eyes. "Does the idea of having my baby completely disgust and horrify you?"

"I think that's what's called a loaded question."

"Do you hate the idea of having a baby?"

"No." She sniffs, wetly. "I mean... it's not something I ever thought would happen... but... no, I don't hate the idea. I... I quite like babies."

"Yeah. So do I."

Jase leans forward and kisses her forehead.

"Oh, Jase. I know what you're thinking. You're thinking about the person you wish you were having this conversation with. I'm so sorry."

She puts her arms around him, enfolding him in a desperate, shuddering embrace. Jase wonders at the speed with which the world has become an entirely different place.

They return to the studio together. The others are listening over to "Fall In Love". "What do you reckon, Jase?" Alun seems to be bothered by something. "It's what you said about the cheese thing. I think I see what you mean."

Ofnadwy Bluesville go back to first positions, and play "It Looks Like I'm Never Gonna Fall In Love Again" one more time. This time, Alun injects a little more desperation into the vocal. Even more startling, though, is Jase's guitar solo, which draws upon the very stuff of his soul, taking on an epic, tragic dimension, to such an extent that Alun almost forgets to come in for his final chorus, so engrossed is he.

Gavin does not appear to notice this, however. "And that, I believe, is a wrap, ladies and gentlemen."

CHAPTER ELEVEN

The painting is magnificent. For one thing, it's big, taking up an embarrassing amount of wall-space, dwarfing the exhibits on either side, one a landscape in monochrome, the other a pointillist nightmare.

Alun is central, naturally enough. He is on one knee, his left arm outstretched in supplication as he gazes skyward, holding the microphone to his snarling lips with a clenched right fist. At the back, Dai's arms are a blur, his eyes wild, his grin devilish. To the left is Lucy, stern and solid, handling her bass with authority; the haircut is severe, but her blouse is undone, displaying a warming cleavage. Jase stands with one foot on the monitor, his hair flying in the breeze, eyes closed, an expression of transcendent bliss on his pale face, the guitar literally an extension of his body. Behind them, the massing clouds are grey, and a single lightning-bolt bisects the frame. "Ofnadwy Bluesville", reads the plate, "Artist: Sonia Raymond."

Jase remembers the photograph it is taken from. The festival in Belgium, where they met Chattanooga Charlie. There was never a thunderstorm, though. And the state of his old dad's knees is such that if he ever chose to drop to them in a cavalier manner, it would take him a good ten minutes to get up again. Furthermore, Jase himself has never been quite as intimate with his guitar as the picture appears to insinuate. Still, it is a highly accomplished piece of work, and, finally seeing it in the flesh, Jase completely understands why the judges thought so highly of it.

"Not bad, eh?"

Jase turns and is pleasantly surprised. "Oh! Hi!" It's Tim, Sonia's boss at the agency. They shake hands.

"Good to see you, Jason. I, er, didn't realise you were still on speaking terms."

"What?"

Tim indicates the painting. "She's been badgering everybody to come and look at it."

"We aren't. I mean… she didn't tell me. I read about it."

It was his mother who had drawn his attention to the feature in the local paper, about the annual exhibition of work by South Wales artists, spread over two floors of St. David's Hall. "Perhaps the most striking of the figurative works featured is a portrait of Valleys-based blues revivalists Ofnadwy Bluesville, painted by a friend of the band."

"So." Jase tries to keep his voice bright. "How is she?"

"Miserable. Well… subdued. But she seems to be cheering up, lately."

"Oh. Good." Jase returns his attention to the painting. "I never even knew she was doing it. She must have wanted it to be a surprise."

"She found out it had been selected just after she came back from holiday."

"Ah." He nods towards the picture. "She hasn't drawn my spots. Must have been in a good mood with me."

"Yeah. She's made you out to be a right rock'n'roll renegade. So, er…" Tim moves in closer. "What happened between you two? She never went into detail."

"What did she say?"

"That you were a bastard. A pathetic one, at that."

This is a stiletto in Jase's heart. "Oh. Right."

Tim has seldom seen a man look so abjectly unhappy. And on the occasions where he has, meddling hasn't helped. "Oh! I heard your record on the radio a couple of days ago! Almost gave me another coronary!"

Jase hasn't really been following the progress of "Fall In Love" / "Nobody's Damn Business". Other things on his mind. "I hope you've placed your order. It's a limited edition kind of thing."

"Oh, I didn't realise."

To be fair, Gavin and Hugo have done them proud. Alun has been monitoring their daily communiqués from his office at the Unaffiliated, and keeping everyone up to date. The local radio stations have been all over it, which is nice, but Hugo has also used his plugging experience to get some national plays, mostly on Radio Two; but there was also the occasion when Tom Jones was being interviewed on Five Live, and they played it to him. "Aye, that's not bad at all, like", he said. Alun did not hear this first time round, and pestered Lucy to find the re-broadcast on the Internet, and record it for him. He plays it every night before he goes to bed.

"Anyway – best be getting back to work"

Tim does a double-take. "Work? Since when do pop-stars need day-jobs?"

"It's a long story." Jase starts to walk away.

"Hey – I'll call you. Fancy doing another session?"

"I… wouldn't Sonia mind?"

"Sonia doesn't run the agency. Yet."

Jase smiles. "That'd be great. Thanks. See you."

The Wednesday after that somewhat eventful weekend in London, Jase was mooching around Cardiff city centre, the cares of the universe weighing him down. Stopping, as was his custom, outside Freddie's, to look over the selection of guitars on display, he noticed the "part-time help wanted" sign in the window. Almost before he knew what was happening, he had wandered in, and was making enquiries. He was pleased when one of the old boys behind the counter recognised him from a Bluesville gig. They were looking for someone to work Mondays to Wednesdays, selling and demonstrating guitars, basses and amps. "I'd like to give it a go", says Jase.

It's been a pleasant couple of weeks. Freddie's has been owned and staffed by pro and semi-pro musicians from the off; the keyboard specialist plays with a Yes tribute band, for instance (which isn't called "Noooo!", as Jase might have suggested), and the man Jase has replaced is away touring Europe as guitar-tech with Tamponika, his girlfriend's tits-out heavy metal combo ("It's not much money, but it's all he can afford!"). Much of the time that isn't taken up with serving customers or arguing good-naturedly about the merits of Jaco Pastorius over Stanley Clarke, is spent fielding outside-work-oriented phone-calls. Thus, Alun's regular communications have already become part of the routine.

"Hey, Dad, you really need to come down and see the painting. It's beautiful."

"Beautiful? With you in it?" But Alun has more pressing matters on his mind. "Now, are you really sure you can't get away tomorrow?"

Tomorrow being the day of the video-shoot. Jase would have been ambivalent in any event, but it coincides with a doctor's appointment for the uneasy parental threesome. "No, I'll be bogged down here all day." His workmates look theatrically from side to side, the store being virtually deserted. They had rocked with laughter when he told them about the situation re Lucy. ("So, you go on holiday with your girlfriend, and the girl you used to fancy, and her lesbian lover – and *which* one's having the baby?"; "Not so much a love triangle – more of a pregnancy polygon!")

"Bloody hell." Alun doesn't sound quite as disappointed as he ought to, somehow. "Lucy can't get away from work, either. Dai's up for it, though."

"Glad to hear it. What's the latest from Gav and Hugo?"

"Oh, you know how it is. It's all chugging along, like."

"Well if that's everything…"

"Erm… there is…" Alun sounds atypically apprehensive. "No, it's okay – we'll talk about it on the weekend. Ciao, kid."

The medical appointment goes smoothly. Dr Akingbola may be young, but she's already seen just about everything, having spent much of her working life thus far in London's excessively vibrant East End.

"The important thing at this stage – well, at every stage – is to avoid stress."

Lucy glances at Carol to her left, and Jase to her right. "The phrase 'easier said than done' comes to mind, Doc."

At least finances aren't an immediate worry. Carol has gone back to bar work, making her mother baby-sit; Jase is still putting in a couple of nights a week with the Khans, in addition to his duties chez Freddie; and Lucy has already organised things with the school so that she will work for as long as possible before the birth (assuming all goes well), and wait until her mind is clearer before deciding whether or not she'll be returning.

Having examined Lucy, and found her to be well, the doctor asks to speak with Jase, alone, for a second.

"You don't look particularly happy, Mr Hopkins. My advice about stress does go for fathers as well."

Jase winces at the f-word. "It's just... a complicated situation. I'll be alright." He smiles, for the first time that day. "Frankly, I'm just starting to look forward to it."

That weekend, Ofnadwy Bluesville embark on what is effectively a nation-wide tour - Friday in Wrexham, Saturday night entertaining students in Aberystwyth, and Sunday lunchtime in Cardiff. Things get off to a bad start when Alun announces, as they are about to set off, that a package containing 200 copies of their CD-single has arrived. "We can sell them, at the gigs, like." The youngsters tear it open, in Christmas-like excitement.

"Ah."

"Right."

"Okay."

The plain navy-blue insert was expected – keeping the costs down. What is a surprise is what is printed on it in red lettering. "Ofnadwy Bluesville featuring Al Hopkins?!"

"Guys, guys, I… I tried, I honestly tried to talk them out of it. But the point they made, and I think it's a fair one, is that the audience needed something to identify with, what with us being an unfamiliar proposition. And, since I'm the singer…"

It is not until they arrive in North Wales, and Alun offers to buy everyone a pub lunch that any of the others talk to him.

"All this has been nothing but a fucking ego-trip for you, hasn't it?!" Lucy is furious.

"Darling – I've been singing in front of paying audiences for more than twenty years. How can you expect me not to have an ego?" Alun decides to go on the offensive. "You should thank me that the band gets a credit at all. They were all set to go with Alun Hopkins' Bluesville."

Jase raises an eyebrow, and takes out his mobile. "What if I call Gavin, and ask him to confirm your story?"

"No, well, when I say… what I mean is… they were all set to drop the 'Ofnadwy' bit. You know – too ethnic."

Jase is aware, from a previous conversation with Hugo and Gavin that the band's name had been an issue, but that Gav was the one who insisted on retaining the Welsh-language element, wary of being labelled a sell-out by his old friend Bryn, with whom he was now on speaking terms once more.

Lucy opens her mouth, about to resume her rant. But she suddenly clamps it shut, covers it with her hand, leaps to her feet, and rushes to the toilet. Jase follows her, and waits outside. She emerges, looking pale.

"Are you okay?"

"I will be." She strokes his arm. "Morning sickness in the afternoon? Trust me to be different."

"Actually, for most women, it happens at all hours of the…"

Lucy raises a hand to shut him up. "Yes, Jason. I know. Carol has been more than forthcoming when it comes to the horrors of childbirth." She smiles. "I'm glad you're doing your revision, though."

When they return to the table, Alun expresses his concern. "Hey – you're not turning into one of them bulimiacs, are you? Trust me – most men like a bit of meat on a woman. Most women, too, from what I can gather."

The Wrexham gig goes well, but Lucy retires to bed early, and Jase joins her. Alun remarks upon the fact that, in the past couple of weeks, Jase has stopped sharing twin rooms with him, and taken to bunking in with Lucy. Just when he should be joining him, out on the prowl. "You're young, free, white and single, boy, you should be out there having a good time."

"Having a good time is over-rated, Dad."

It isn't until Lucy faints in the dressing-room, prior to the Aberystwyth show, while Jase is off looking at the sea, that Alun gets an inkling. He rushes out to find a medic, and stays with Lucy as her vital signs are checked. "How many weeks gone is she?"

Alun looks blankly from the doctor, to Dai, to the recovering Lucy. "You what?"

"Nine, ten", says Dai, doing a passable impression of a responsible adult.

"Were you ever going to tell me?!" thunders Alun, when Jase has returned, and established that Lucy is fine.

"We thought you might eventually figure it out for yourself."

"Don't you cheek me, boy!" Alun's vehemence shakes them all. "If I'm going to be a fucking grand-dad, I want to fucking know about it."

"Watch your language in front of the baby, mun." Dai grins, impish.

"It's... its not straightforward, Dad."

"Yeah, you got that right." Alun sits, head in hands. "How could you be so stupid?"

"Dad – we've been through all this."

"And you!" Alun turns to Lucy. "You're supposed to be the intelligent one round here!"

"Reports of my intelligence have been grossly exaggerated." She smiles at him. "We've got over the panic phase, Alun. We're being grown-ups, now."

She sees the Aber gig through without further mishap, but Alun finally understands why the others insisted on booking an overnight stay rather than taking the southbound road overnight. Unusually, the four of them spend their pre-bedtime leisure hours together, talking about the future. Lucy insists that she'll be well able to fulfil her concert commitments well into her third trimester, but that beyond that… "Well, maybe you should start looking around for a new bass-player." The others insist that without Lucy, Ofnadwy Bluesville would no longer be Ofnadwy Bluesville. Lucy bursts into tears.

The promotional video for "Fall In Love", when it finally hits the streets, is commonly held to be something of a classic. Shot in a single day by a student crew, friends of Gavin's from Mid-Wales, it starts with Dai, in a tuxedo and clown make-up, executing a Restoration Comedy bow, as he opens the door of the Unaffiliated's function suite, to reveal Alun, sitting, disconsolate upon the stage, his tie undone, beckoning the camera towards him before starting to sing. Later sequences see him strolling disconsolately along the brow of a windswept hill; disconsolately throwing stones into the sea at Barry Island; sitting in the park, disconsolately watching as a young couple (the director's sister and her boyfriend) stroll by hand-in-hand; and disconsolately mooching around an art gallery, pausing and stroking his chin, in front of Sonia's painting of Ofnadwy Bluesville. The camera zooms in on the guitarist, whereupon there is a dissolve into footage of the band playing at the summer rock festival, featuring close-ups of Jase playing solos on a number of entirely different songs, and slow-motion shots of the wild-man drummer, the boyishly sexy bassist with her bouncing breasts, and the singer, the very picture of pensiveness. When the instrumental break ends, we return to Alun, sauntering through the city streets, grimacing bravely. He bumps into Dai, who greets him warmly, and the final shot is of the two of them marching into a pub to drown their manly sorrows.

The first time it crops up on VH1, Jase, his mother and Jefferson are open-mouthed in the front room. As it fades, they are afraid to look at one another, until Jefferson catches the horrified expression on Violet's face, and explodes into laughter. Within seconds, the three of them are rolling about, blinded by tears of mirth, Violet remarking that this is the first occasion in a quarter of a century where that man has provoked any emotion in her other than heartache.

When Jase next leaves the house, he makes sure to wear his dark glasses.

"Oi. Clown Boy." This is as Dai is wandering home, after an evening of being bought drinks by people who, a month ago, would have been unwilling even to acknowledge that they knew him. It is less than a week before Ofnadwy Bluesville's "Fall In Love" is to be unleashed on an undeserving public. The video, and Dai's dual role within it, are something of a local talking point; thus jibes relating to clown-hood are no longer a novelty. "Oi. I'm talking to you!"

"Oh. Hi, guys." Dai greets the encroaching Bumpy and Teg as though they were former, vague acquaintances.

"We, er, haven't seen you in a while." Teg seems hurt.

"Well, you know how it is. Busy, busy, busy." The truth being that Dai has found a new source, in Cardiff, who treats him with marginally less contempt.

"Seen you on the telly", says Bumpy.

"That must be nice for you."

"We hear your record's doing quite well." Teg smiles, grimly. "Going into the top twenty, they say."

"Can't believe everything you read, Teg, mun." Dai is glancing around him, scoping out an exit route. "Anyway, do you know how few records you have to sell to get into the charts these days? It's a scandal."

"Still – not bad going."

"No, no, not bad at all, like."

"The thing is, David – you owe us a considerable amount of money."

Dai giggles. "You what?"

"You heard him." Bumpy clumsily rubs the fingers or one hand together in the well-worn gesture. "We've been doing our sums."

"Thought I hadn't seen you out for a while."

"It's amazing how these debts tend to creep up on you from behind, though."

"Yeah, Teg, Fascinating. Anyway." He turns, and starts to walk away. He is unsurprised when they catch up with him, walking one on either side.

"You owe us, Williams."

"So you said."

"I'm serious."

"I'll pay you when I get my wages."

"It runs into thousands, Dai. You could have knocked us over with a feather when we totted it up."

"Teg. Listen to me – you know how much I earn doing gigs. It's beer-money. Okay, so I'm in a video – shock news – we don't get paid for that. Effectively, we're paying them. Okay, so we've made a record. It gets played on the radio. People might buy it. But did I write the song? No. I'm just an employee. So I'm not going to be bathing in hundred-pound notes any time soon. Okay?"

Bumpy grabs Dai's shoulder, causing him to stop dead. "That doesn't change the fact that you owe us."

"Oh, fuck off, will you?!"

Teg looks at Bumpy. Bumpy looks at Teg. They both look at Dai. "I beg your pardon!"

"You've had your fun, guys. The amount of shit you've put me through, this past few years? The things you've done to me? I don't owe you donkey-fucking jam-rags a bastard penny!"

Before any of them quite realise what is happening, Bumpy has got Dai in a headlock, and is dragging him into the car-park of his least favourite pub. Dai strikes out with his foot, managing to catch Teg a good one in the gonads. Bumpy slams Dai's face into the bonnet of a grey Volvo, and lets him drop to the ground. Teg leaps on him, landing knees-first on his chest, and rams his forehead into Dai's nose, causing it to explode in a shower of redness. He then grabs Dai's left fore-arm, and lays it flat on the floor, enabling Bumpy whom, lest we forget, is not a small man, to perform a flamenco flourish on Dai's hand, in his size thirteen retro Doc Marten boots. Teg then rolls the screaming Dai over onto his front, grabbing his right wrist and repeating the procedure. This time, Bumpy contents himself with a basic stomping motion with one foot, stopping when it starts to feel like he's treading in jelly. By this time, Dai is squealing like a slit baby pig.

Teg climbs to his feet, breathing heavily. "Okay. *Now* you've paid your fucking debt."

Bumpy and Teg walk away, content with a job well done.

"And coming up in part two, the latest Welsh act destined to make a dent in the hit parade – but this time, there's a twist!"

In the days leading up to the release of "Fall In Love", Alun appears on all three local daily news magazines programmes, on consecutive days. The BBC settle for a brief interview with him at his desk in the Unaffiliated ("I'm delighted, frankly, it's what my career's been leading up to all these years!"), a clip of the video, and some words from a music journalist, bemoaning the devalued currency of pop hit status. S4C up the ante by getting him into the studio, alongside Gavin, who bigs up the achievements of his record company, with Alun getting a few well-rehearsed Welsh phrases in; they also show a clip of Ofnadwy Bluesville which they've discovered in their archives – from a festival in North Wales, where they'd played in the summer; it had not previously been broadcast because the station was concentrating on Welsh-speaking acts.

It is HTV Wales which truly does Alun proud, devoting an entire segment to him and him alone.

"… and the lead singer of Ofnadwy Bluesville is here with us right now, Alun Hopkins, how are you?"

"I'm fine, Lucy, delighted to be here."

"It's a slightly unusual story, isn't it, the story of Ofnadwy Bluesville?"

"Well, I guess you could say that. Erm, I've been singing in the clubs for, well, several years now, but I was taking a bit of a break from that, and my son, Jason…"

"The guitarist."

"That's right, Lucy, yes; erm, he suggested that he and I should form a blues band, pooling our diverse talents, as it were."

"And you've done quite well as a live act, I hear."

"Well, yes, it all came together pretty quickly, and we discovered that there was this established touring circuit for blues type acts, and…" At this point, he is quite clearly looking down her blouse. "…well, we hopped on the bandwagon, you might say."

"And now it looks as though you're going to have a top twenty single."

"Yes, it's amazing, really, Lucy; a friend of my son's, who used to be in quite a well-known band, he runs a label now, and he saw us play and decided that he might be able to do something with us."

"A classic by Tom Jones – sacrilege, some might say!"

"Well, all respect to Tom, but we've put our own unique spin on it."

"Well, you certainly have! Erm… the video's an interesting one…"

"Erm... sorry, can I just..."

"I'm sorry?"

"It's just... our drummer, Dai, he was involved in a bit of an incident last night, and he's in hospital..."

"Goodness! I hope he's alright!"

"Well, apparently it was a bit dicey for a while, but it looks like he's on the mend, now; anyway, I just wanted to say hello to him, and the rest of the guys..."

"They couldn't join you this evening..."

"No, I... well, our bass-player's pregnant, so she's resting..."

"Well, congratulations to her!"

"Er, yes, and, erm, Jase, my boy, well, he's a bit on the shy side, like..."

"Bastard!" Cut to Jase, at Dai's hospital bedside. It was nothing to do with being shy; more an issue of not wanting to look like a plonker, miming his guitar solo in his father's swaggering shadow. "I told him, we could do an acoustic version. But he says no, people want to hear it the way it is on the record! Tosser!"

"Leave him be, mun." Dai is sounding more than slightly nasal. "Moment of glory, innit?"

"Yeah, but... he's making me out like some sort of hermit."

"Man of mystery, mun." Dai sniffs, and cringes, since it hurts.

On the television, Alun is starting to sing "Fall In Love", mercifully to the Ofnadwy Bluesville backing-track, and not some effort cobbled together by the telly people. He gazes soulfully into the eyes of the viewer one second, looking bashfully away the next, working it like the pro he always was. The credits start to roll as Jase's virtuoso guitar part begins.

"Bugger! My solo!"

"They certainly have", says Dai, as the adverts kick in.

"Ah, well." Jase sighs, as he returns his attention to the broken face of his best friend. "Still, at least he gave you a shout-out."

"Yeah. That was nice of the old fucker."

Jase gets up. "I'm off to the toilet. Can I bring you anything back?"

"From the toilet? No, you're alright, mate."

"Daft sod." Jase gently tweaks Dai's toe. "Back in a sec."

Left alone, Dai allows himself to die a little. Ever since regaining consciousness, he's felt low, and it's not just the pain. Or the withdrawal. Ever since he was small, he's always landed on his feet, always felt a sense of invulnerability. That's why he's spent so much of his life testing the limits. Like in that film Jase once dragged him to see, where they run through a dense forest, blindfolded, so they can get a buzz out of coming out the other side, totally unscathed. At this moment, for the first time in years, he feels… scathed. And stupid.

"Dai?"

He hasn't yet seen what the new, mashed-up Dai looks like. But the expressions on the faces of his visitors are as telling as any mirror.

"Sonia! Long time no see!"

She glides in, forcing a smile, a tad too late. "Oh, Dai – what have you done to yourself?"

"You should see the other fella! Ouch." This is as she kisses his forehead.

"Sorry."

"Didn't hurt. I was just trying to freak you out, like."

"Dai – all you've ever had to do to freak me out is just be Dai." She sits in Jase's chair. "I kept phoning. They said you'd been in intensive care all night."

"Bloody Health Service. Always exaggerating. I was never going to die, or anything."

"But… your hands. Your beautiful hands."

Dai glances down at the mess of splints and bloody bandages. "I didn't know you cared."

And suddenly, Jase is back, frozen in the doorway. "Sonia."

"Jase. Hi."

"Hi." A silence as they take one another in. "I, er, liked your painting."

"Oh. Thanks."

"What? The painting that made me out to be some kind of drug-crazed nutter?" Dai struggles to try and face Sonia. "I'll have you know, I'm considering legal action."

"So, er, how've you been?"

Jase shrugs. "Not that good. How about you?"

"Same. I guess."

"I should have asked for a Tom Cruise."

They both look at Dai.

"What?"

"When I came in. The busted nose. People pay thousands to get their noses broken and made into different shapes, like. If I'd been conscious I could have asked for a Cruise."

Sonia smiles. "Well, at least you're keeping cheerful."

"It's these painkillers they've got me on. Seriously – I may never go back to the other stuff!"

But Jase and Sonia have already resumed their staring contest.

"Erm… congratulations. On the record. Both of you."

"Cheers. Oh, er, thanks for letting us use it in the video. The painting."

"No worries." Another silence. "Lucy wrote and told me. About the baby."

"Oh. Right." Jase lowers his eyes. "At least something good might come out of… you know. Something that means something."

A nurse peeps in, past Jase. She clocks Dai's exasperation. "I think Mr Williams has had enough excitement for one day."

"Right." Jase comes fully into the room, smiles at Dai, bends down and kisses his forehead.

"What is it with my forehead lately? Fucking irresistible, or what?"

"It's the only part of your face anyone can get to, mate."

"Oh, yeah."

As Jase glances back at him on leaving the room, he catches a glimpse of the deflated, unhappy Dai, which makes him want to cry.

Jase and Sonia do not say another word until they are in the lobby of the hospital. "Well, it was good to see you, Sonia."

"I could… do you want a lift back to the station?"

"Actually, that'd be really useful." Looking at her eyebrows, he notices some white hairs that weren't there before. "Thanks."

As they stroll out to the car-park, Jase manages to stammer the question he's been dying to ask. "So, are you… are you seeing anybody?"

"Not at the moment."

"Oh. So you… have been seeing people."

"Been on a couple of dates."

"Oh. Any good ones?"

"Nothing to write home about. How about you?"

"Nah. Been too busy. You know how it is."

"Sure do."

They don't speak again until they are in the front seat of her car. Their hands accidentally touch as they're doing up their seatbelts. "Sorry."

Sonia starts to turn the key in the ignition, then stops. "What did you mean?"

"What?"

"What did you mean? When you said you didn't deserve to be forgiven?"

"Oh." He examines a speck of dust on the windscreen. "I think… I'm starting to realise that I'm more like my dad than I ever thought I was. Just as selfish, just as insensitive. It just comes out in different ways, that's all. If we'd stuck together, I'd only have hurt you again. And if I did, and you forgave me… I might start to… you know. Respect you less."

Sonia sits, immobile for several seconds. "One of the dates I went on… it was with a mate of Tim's, from work. Older guy. Younger than Tim, but… old enough. Works in network solutions, whatever the fuck that is, he did explain. And we're having quite a nice evening, he knows a lot about stuff, you know, art, films, Internet stuff. And towards the end of the evening, as he gets drunker and drunker, he starts going on about how he'd really like to show me his technique. His oral sex technique. And he wiggles his tongue in my face. And I laugh it off, you know, dirty old man, not on a first date, all that kind of stuff. But, anyway, we get a taxi back to mine, and I ask him in for coffee. And he's starting to sober up a little, and there's this look in his eye. And I say, what the hell. And I let him."

"Oh." Jase has to clear his throat. "That must have been very interesting for you."

Without warning, Sonia puts her hand on his crotch. "Aha. Erection."

"What does that prove?"

"That you aren't as angelic as you like everybody to think you are. That's not the reason you let me go so easily. It's just that you'd rather wallow in misery than face the truth. That love… and life, come to think about it… it's about hurting people, and being hurt, and waking up the next day and getting on with it."

Jase lifts her hand, and places it on her knee. "So is that what you want? You want me to be a bastard? Because that's what all women want? Fair enough, Sonia. But that's not me. Take me to the station, please."

But she doesn't take him to the station. She takes him back to her flat. Where they have desperate, hungry, almost-fully-clothed sex on her sofa. Then they drink herbal tea and eat biscuits, and talk about work, and friends, and the future. And then they go to bed, like grown-ups.

CHAPTER TWELVE

"Fall In Love / Nobody's Damn Business" by Ofnadwy Bluesville (featuring Alun Hopkins) enters the Official Top 40 at number 6. The following week, it falls to number 11. The week after that - Christmas week, when more singles are sold than at any other period - it rises to number 9. Its trajectory then goes as follows: 12, 27, 36, and out, although it remains in the Top 75 until March, the whole limited edition thing having been something of a scam. Thanks to Hugo's B-side brainwave, everybody manages to wind up with brass in pocket, even after the Inland Revenue has discovered their home addresses.

It is Alun who drinks most deeply from the trough of impermanent celebrity. By the end of January, his friends estimate that he has been on every single programme on terrestrial and satellite television which both welcomes guests and requires them to keep their clothes on. He walks down the red carpet at the London premieres of two middling Hollywood movies; presents the trophy for Best Album (alongside a palpably fake-breasted teenage soap starlet) at a minor music awards ceremony; and is mercilessly lampooned by his team-mates on a prime-time comedy panel-show. It is only when he, and his new thousand-quid suit, are covered in a barrel-full of viscous green goo, live on Children's BBC, that he decides to cut his losses and return home.

He shocks everybody, including himself, by turning down an ostensibly huge recording deal, reasoning correctly, that they would have tried to tailor him for the grannies' market, and have him crooning in the Perry Como / Andy Williams style. "I mean, respect to them both, like, but that's not me." He estimates that his long-term earnings, and mental health, will be enhanced if he concentrates on live work. He engages a shit-hot showbiz agent, resigns from the Unaffiliated, and goes on the road, building on the credibility points amassed by the Bluesville by selling himself as a specialist in vintage blues and soul, soft-pedalled for the mature audience. He finds himself doing very, very, very well.

Whilst playing in Dublin, he arranges to meet Miriam, the woman he got it together with in Amsterdam. They get it together again, and he accidentally invites her to come and visit him in Wales. Not having much going for her in Ireland any more, she takes him up on his offer, turning up on his door-step one drizzly Tuesday evening. She never leaves.

Lucy gives birth to Elmore Jay Tyson (3.8 kg), without mishap, on the cusp of spring and summer. Both Jase and Carol are present at the birth, but only one of them bursts into tears when the midwife announces that his new son appears to be perfect.

Everyone falls in love with little Elmore on first sight, even Sonia, who had been hoping to retain her objectivity. Alun remarks on the baby's good fortune in taking, looks-wise, after his mother rather than his father.

Her Bluesville earnings mean that Lucy doesn't have to worry about returning to work, at least in the short term. Her brain appears to have turned to mush, in any case. She formulates a vague plan involving going into teacher-training when Elmore reaches school age, but decides to keep her options open; after all, looking after Carol and the two babies is virtually a full-time job in itself. She even goes entire months without touching her bass guitar, which has never happened before. Still, she supposes that it's all part of having a life.

Thanks to the fact that he's completely unable to use his hands for several weeks, Dai finds himself in something of a default detoxification scenario, at least as far as the heroin is concerned. While this is far from symptomless, the painkillers appear to help a great deal, to the extent that he is surprised that, when they start to wind down his medication, this doesn't bother him, over-much.

It's not that he wakes up one morning and declares himself free of drugs. He simply decides that he may as well seize the opportunity to see what else is out there.

He is peeved when he realises that he has only fuzzy memories of a brief but successful career in the music business. Despite the physiotherapy, and his natural robustness, it quickly becomes clear that he will never again be able to play drums at world-class level, although he's still able to dabble. Fiddling with car-parts, another source of enjoyment, is also something of a struggle. With his Bluesville money, he buys himself a mobile home and, having seen Elmore safely into the world, sets off to drive around Europe, having crazy adventures. Although, in this case, "Europe" means France and Spain, and he winds up spending most of his time in Malaga, before returning to seek treatment for what turns out to be an infestation of pubic lice, picked up from a middle-aged German woman who was also seeking adventure.

"You want to be a what?", asks Jase, eyes bulging in disbelief.

"A drugs counsellor."

"No, Dai – I think you're misunderstanding the entire concept. The job of a drugs counsellor is not to advise people on where to get the best drugs."

"You're a funny man, anyone ever tell you that?"

Despite Jase's scepticism, Dai makes enquiries, and realises that's it's entirely practicable for him to use his experiences to help other addicts to recover. He also advertises his services as a peripatetic percussion teacher, and rapidly finds himself over-subscribed. Which at least allows him to take an occasional break from the depression which is, his doctor informs him, a natural consequence of having spent several years sodomizing his brain.

One of the many things Sonia tells Jase, during their first night of being back together, is that she has been offered a job in the design department of a large record company in London, partly on the basis of her painting having been used in the Ofnadwy Bluesville video. Jase tells her that, of course, she mustn't turn it down on his account, but that he's not going anywhere, not with a baby on the way.

"I'm not going to be like my Dad. I'm going to be there for my child. Whether they want me there or not."

When she phones the company to decline their kind offer, she is informed that things can easily be arranged so that she can do most of her work at home, only coming into the office once or twice a week. In fact, every objection she makes is countered by their throwing more incentives at her (company discounts on CDs, broadband internet installation), to the extent that she feels obligated to accept.

Tim is sorry to lose her, but a high staff turnover is inherent to the advertising game, and there are no bad feelings. On the contrary, when she mentions that she would like to get into portrait-painting, he slips some of his high-powered Taffia friends her number, and she gets some very useful commissions.

Sonia and Jase are both slightly suspicious when their relationship appears to have resumed almost as though they'd been apart for a mere day or two, rather than several bitter weeks during which they did not communicate at all, during which they each put themselves through several kinds of hell. But then they've both been brought up, in their different ways, to believe that if it doesn't hurt, it can't be doing you any good. And in very short order they come to accept that maybe, just maybe, a feeling of happiness doesn't always necessarily signal imminent disaster.

Thus, they move in together, into a rented two-bedroomed flat in Cardiff, not far from Sonia's previous residence. It is a curiously stress-free experience, apart from the dozens of self-replicating cardboard boxes. One Thursday evening, they're talking on the 'phone, him taking a break from burnt rice and micro-waved cod fillets at his Mum's, her with her "Sex And The City"

DVD on pause; the next Thursday evening, they're living together, making fresh pasta in their new wood-panelled kitchen, and arguing over the merits of Jean-Luc Godard.

Jase continues to make music, obviously – it is he who puts together his father's live backing tapes. He leaves Freddie's, secure in the knowledge that he can pop back anytime for a chat about wah-wah pedals with his mates. Tim starts to employ his services on a fairly regular basis, and he also gets to play on a couple of records put out by Hugo and Gavin – one an attempt at girl-gang pop, the other the debut by a new Asian soul-singing sensation, both of which are moderate hits. Fiddling around with some electronic equipment in which he's invested, Jase finds himself developing some interesting variants on guitar-oriented hard-core dance music, and puts out a single of his own, which sells well enough, but is denied official Top 40 access, due to its inordinate length.

By the time Miriam invites everyone round for a celebration of Alun's 48th birthday, which roughly coincides with the first anniversary of Ofnadwy Bluesville's record deal being signed, they are all able to muse together on the extent to which their lives have changed for the better. Violet does not attend, of course, and Sonia casts Lucy the occasional dark glance, but otherwise, it is a genial Bluesville family occasion, with much laughter, moderate drinking, and minimal grandstanding from Al, as he sings Bobby Womack songs with Jase on guitar, and Dai on light bongo duties. Lucy is too busy cleaning up baby-sick to feel overly nostalgic. A moment does come to mind, though, which seems to encapsulate the whole experience.

It is from the gig they played at the Stoke Sugarmill, around ten days after their frantic Welsh tour weekend. This is Ofnadwy Bluesville's final performance, although they haven't yet acknowledged the fact to one another. The single, which is about to be released, is all over the radio – even "Nobody's Damn Business" has received a couple of plays - and the last of the batch they've been selling at gigs has been snapped up while the support band was doing their thing. There is, needless to say, a capacity crowd.

They are in the middle of "Blues In The Night". Alun is hanging back, as Jase plays his solo. And Dai is plainly both off his face and treading water, this not being a song which heavily features the drums; and Jase has been hassling Lucy all evening, and is still sorely missing Sonia; and Al is only pretending to watch his son, as he eyes up some well-upholstered totty in the front row who has already rebuffed his advances; and Lucy herself is pretty sure she's going to be howling into the toilet-bowl within the hour.

But they all have ridiculously stupid smiles on their faces.

Lightning Source UK Ltd.
Milton Keynes UK
UKOW050735240911

179220UK00001B/301/P